"Don't look at me. Go away. Please go away."

He laid her down on the bed and went over to the wall-to-wall fitted wardrobe. He pulled out a warm blue wool dressing gown and brought it back to her.... She was far too thin, but she was hauntingly lovely.

"How can you do such stupid things to yourself?" he asked her. "You don't need to diet, you have a beautiful body. Why are you trying to destroy it for the sake of vanity?"

Dear Reader,

The Seven Deadly Sins are those sins that most of us are in danger of committing every day: very ordinary failings, very human weaknesses, which can cause pain both to ourselves and others. Over the ages they have been defined as: Anger, Covetousness, Envy, Greed, Lust, Pride and Sloth.

In this book I deal with the sin of Greed. Sometimes what appears to be greed can, in fact, be an unbearable need that has run out of control. You can forgive someone who is only harming themselves; it is different when someone's greed to possess turns to crime and hurts other people.

Charlotte Lamb

This is the fourth story in Charlotte Lamb's gripping series. Watch out for three more romances—all complete stories in themselves—in which this exceptionally talented writer proves that love can conquer the deadliest of sins!

Coming next month: DARK FEVER (Harlequin Presents #1840)...the sin of Lust.

ALSO AVAILABLE IN HARLEQUIN PRESENTS SINS

Charlotte Lamb

Wild Hunger

Harlequin Books

TORONTO • NEW YORK • LONDON
AMSTERDAM • PARIS • SYDNEY • HAMBURG
STOCKHOLM • ATHENS • TOKYO • MILAN
MADRID • WARSAW • BUDAPEST • AUCKLAND

ISBN 0-373-11834-1

WILD HUNGER

First North American Publication 1996.

Copyright © 1995 by Charlotte Lamb.

Printed in U.S.A.

CHAPTER ONE

GERARD FINDLAY was watching his fax machine roll out another irritated message from his news editor when he heard the screaming.

The noise took him back nearly three months, to the moments that haunted his sleep every night. He began to shake, waiting for the machine-gun fire, the deafening thud of rockets landing on their target, the smell of burning, the clouds of brick dust rising in the air, then his mind cleared and he remembered where he was, realised what he was hearing.

The noise came from the house next door and he was safe in London.

'Those girls! Those damned girls!' he said through his teeth, angrily aware of the perspiration trickling down his back. 'One day I'll wring their necks!'

From the day, six months ago, that he'd moved into a little mews cottage a stone's throw from Chelsea Bridge he had been driven mad by the girls who lived next door. They were either having a party, playing loud pop music or yelling at each other from room to room. He had banged on the wall, gone next door to complain, and got no-where. In the end, he had complained to the agent who had rented him his cottage.

'One of them is the owner's stepdaughter,' the agent wryly told him. 'The redhead.'

'Oh, her,' Gerard had said, remembering a girl who walked like a dancer, tall, slender, amazingly graceful, with a mop of vivid red hair and green eyes that reminded him of the slanting stare of an angry cat.

The agent had grinned at him. 'Easy on the eye, isn't she? Mind you, so is her friend, with the long black hair. They're both models, you know.'

Incredulously, he had said, 'You mean there are only two of them? There always seems to be a whole mob in the place!'

The agent had laughed indulgently. 'You know what young people are like! Partying day and night. Look, I'll report your complaint, but I can't promise anything will come of it.'

Gerard had no idea how the landlord had taken his complaint. He had been unexpectedly dispatched next day, with a camera team, to cover a civil war in what had once been a peaceful little country, when the team who had been out there for some time showed signs of battle fatigue. It was unwise to leave them under strain of that kind for too long; their reports always deteriorated. Gerard himself had felt the strain before long, although he had only been in the war zone for a matter of weeks.

When he'd got back home from the hospital he'd noticed that the only tenant of the tiny cottage next door was now the owner's stepdaughter, the redhead who moved as if she danced every step she took. Every time they saw each other, coming or going, she ignored him in a very pointed, icy fashion.

It was obvious that she knew he had complained to the agent about her and her friend, and she resented it. Had her stepfather blamed the other girl, the dark-haired one? And asked her to leave? Gerard felt guilty about that; he had rather liked the dark girl. When he'd first moved in, she had come round with sandwiches and a pot of good coffee while his removal firm was shifting furniture around. The removal men had been wide-eyed and fascinated. When she had gone they had wolf-whistled and said, 'You lucky man, you! We'll move in with you, with neighbours like that. Did you see her legs? Wow.'

Gerard might have been more interested, himself, if he hadn't just quarrelled with a girl he had been dating for months. He had discovered that while he was abroad for weeks Judy usually dated other men, and Gerard resented it.

'You mean you never stray while you're away?' Judy had been cynically incredulous and when he'd insisted that he didn't she just wouldn't believe him. It had been the end of the affair. He had been badly hurt, jealous every time he imagined her with another man. It had left Gerard too sore to want to get involved with anyone else just yet.

The dark girl had invited him to one of their parties, the following weekend, but he had been busy and had forgotten all about it. The next time they bumped into each other coming or going from the mews she had softly reproached him. He had made his excuses, and she had relented gracefully. 'Well, I forgive you this time! Look, we're having another party next Saturday—try and come this time!'

'I'm sorry, I'm just off to Brazil,' he had said, smiling wryly back.

'For TV?' she had asked, admitting tacitly that she knew who he was—and Gerard had stiffened up. Were they inviting him because he was a celebrity, his face on TV every night, in the news? Gerard didn't enjoy celebrity. He was a reporter, not an entertainer. He hated it when people were friendly to him simply because his face came into their homes every night. When he'd worked on a newspaper he had never got that sort of reaction. Newspaper reporters were anonymous, faceless people, on the whole. Nobody recognised you; when they found out what you did they were usually indifferent, unless they had an axe to grind about some report you had filed on them or their relatives.

'That's right.' Irritated, he added, 'By the way, can you and your friend keep the noise down in the evenings? I have to get to bed early and you seem to be up half the night playing rock music. It's giving me a headache.'

She had looked at him sweetly. 'Sure.'

They hadn't, of course. In fact, he had a strong impression that they had turned up the volume after that, and they had stopped inviting him to their parties. If Gerard banged on the wall the volume went up even higher. If he went round to remonstrate with them the redhead looked at him as if he were a slug which was eating her lettuce.

A sudden hammering on his own front door made him jump. For a moment he couldn't move, paralysed by shock. Oh, pull yourself together! he told himself contemptuously. This isn't the Civil War; you're back home again, in London, safe. Aren't you the lucky one? What if you were still there?

His doorbell was ringing, loudly and persist-
ently; someone had their finger pressed down on
it. 'Hello?' someone called through the letter-box.
'Oh, please be in, please...help me!'

Gerard made it to the door, pulled it open, his
black brows jerking together in a scowl which made
the girl outside back away instinctively for a second.

Gerard was a formidable sight: a big man, lean
and sinewy, muscular but light on his feet when he
had to move fast. He was a squash player, swam
every day, when he had time he worked out at the
gym near his newspaper office and quite often
walked a good deal of the way to work, unless he
was in a tearing hurry.

'I'm—I'm sorry to bother you,' stammered the
girl on his doorstep.

'You're the girl who moved out!' he said, recognising her.

'Sara Ounissi,' she said, nodding, but she was
too upset for polite chat. 'Please, I need your help,'
she added pleadingly. Her accent was foreign,
although her English was very good. The name
sounded Arabic. She had told him her name
before—he was sure it hadn't been Ounissi, though.

'What's wrong?' he asked, resisting when she
tried to pull him out of his home by the hand. He
suspected a fight between the two girls and didn't
want to get involved.

'I have to get into the cottage; she won't let me
in, but I know she's there—I heard her moaning.
I'm afraid she'll die this time.'

'Die?' he repeated, taken aback. What had the
two girls been fighting over? A man? This one
looked so gentle: slightly built, although like her

friend she was tall, with elegantly long-fingered hands and slender feet, hair the colour of jet, smooth skin, with a soft, golden sheen, her great, dark eyes like a doe's, liquid and sweet.

'Please come; don't waste time asking questions,' she wailed. 'I've been trying to get her to answer, but she won't.'

'Maybe she isn't in?'

'Oh, yes, she is in there; I tell you I have heard her.'

'You've quarrelled with her?'

'No, no, you don't understand...she's very upset. She lost her TV contract this morning, a big advertising campaign, for Rexel, the cosmetics firm. Keira has been their "face" for the past year; you must have seen her on TV, putting on their make-up?'

His mouth twisted. 'I rarely have time to watch TV.' For the past three years he had been out of the country more often than he had been in it, and when he was at home the only programmes he watched were news and current affairs programmes.

'But you are on TV every night!' The dark eyes reproached him, accused him of hypocrisy, double standards. 'TV is your business!'

'Only the news!' People increasingly confused news and entertainment, and it annoyed Gerard. He and his colleagues spilt their blood getting the news back to this country from war-torn parts of the world, and people watched as if it were all another adventure film, the blood just make-up. 'And if I do catch a programme I never watch the advertisements,' he said impatiently. 'While they're on I get myself a drink.'

The dark girl shrugged. 'Well, Rexel is a big cosmetics firm and the contract was worth a lot of money. Her contract was up for renewal this week—and without warning they dropped her.'

'That's tough luck. I suppose she'll miss the money? But aren't her family wealthy? She won't starve, surely? It can't be a matter of life and death——'

Sara Ounissi interrupted fiercely, 'That isn't the point.' She made a frustrated gesture with those long, delicate hands. 'Keira takes rejections hard; they can trigger a violent mood swing. Her agent rang me to warn me she was devastated about suddenly being dropped by Rexel. Benny was my agent too; that's why he rang me—I used to model. Fashion mostly—for magazines.' She gave him an instinctive, faintly flirtatious look through her long, dark lashes. 'Maybe you noticed me in one some time? But I gave it up when I got married last month. My husband doesn't want me to go on modelling.'

Gerard's brows rose; the women he worked with wouldn't take kindly to being told to give up work by their husbands. 'And you don't mind that?'

She gave him a cool, dignified glance which resented the question. 'His lifestyle will mean that I have a great deal to do at home; I wouldn't have time to model as well. We travel a good deal; he has homes in Switzerland, the Gulf and Sussex. Luckily that was where I was this week. It took me ages to get up to London, and now she won't let me in. I've been banging and calling for ages. I must get into the cottage—I suppose your key wouldn't fit her front door?'

'I hope not,' Gerard said curtly. 'I certainly wouldn't want her letting herself in here whenever I'm away.'

The dark girl made an angry, spitting noise. 'Oh, for the love of heaven! Don't you get it? This is an emergency!'

He considered her, frowning. 'What are you afraid of? Losing a job may be a bad blow, but it won't make her suicidal unless she's neurotic.'

'You don't understand. Keira...has a problem...'

Gerard's mouth twisted contemptuously. 'I see. Drugs.' His tone was scathing now. 'You're afraid she's taken an overdose?'

'No!' the girl said explosively. 'She's ill; she has bulimia... Now do you see?'

He looked blank. 'Bulimia? That isn't life-threatening. It's just the opposite of anorexia, isn't it?'

'I thought you were a journalist?' It was Sara's turn to be scornful. 'You should know about bulimia; it can be just as serious as anorexia. She eats and eats, and then deliberately makes herself sick. Eventually that can cause internal bleeding; she could be unconscious in there, could have choked to death. Since I moved out I haven't been able to keep an eye on her; I don't know what's been going on.' The girl stared at him, her face angry and desperate. 'Look, if you won't help, can I use your phone to call the police? There isn't time to argue with you. I have to get to her.'

'I'm sorry,' Gerard said. 'OK, then, why don't we ring the owner? Isn't he her stepfather?'

Sara's face tightened. Gerard got the feeling she didn't like the owner of the cottage. 'He's in Tangier.'

'Hasn't she got any other family?'

'Not in this country.'

'Oh. Well, we could ring the agent and ask if he has a key.'

The dark girl's face lit up. 'I should have thought of that! He's just around the corner. I'll go right away.'

'Hang on, we should ring first—I'll find his number.' Gerard went back into his own cottage, with the dark girl on his heels, looked up the number, rang the agent's office and spoke to his secretary.

'He's out at present. We do have a key, of course. Did you say Sara was there? Could she come here to pick it up?'

The dark-haired girl had been listening. 'I'll go,' she said, and was gone, running.

He told the secretary she was coming and rang off. The fax machine was chattering again; he let the latest screed from his editor drop into the tray awaiting it, glanced at it, sighing. It was another refusal to send him abroad on a story. 'Come into the office. I need to talk to you,' it ended.

Gerard screwed it up and threw it across the room, then went out into the cobbled mews.

A hundred years ago horses had been stabled in these little gabled buildings which had been built at the back of gardens belonging to the big Victorian houses lining the streets on either side of the alley. After the Second World War the stables had all been converted into dwellings. They were highly sought after; painted in bright colours, each one had a window-box for a garden. Gerard's house had a scarlet-enamelled front door with a brass lion's head knocker. The brick walls had been painted cream, and he had planted geraniums in the window-box.

It was a warm afternoon in early summer. The mews was drowsy with heat, the scent of flowers and trees in the gardens behind. Most of the other occupants of the tiny cottages were at work; there were no families here—the houses weren't suitable. Tenants were either single or couples without children.

Gerard climbed on to the windowsill of the ground-floor front room of the cottage next door and peered in at a pretty sitting-room, furnished in spring-like pale green and white. It was empty, and immaculate.

He hoped he wasn't being made a fool—Sara Ounissi might have got the whole thing out of proportion... On the other hand, what if she hadn't? What if the redhead was seriously ill?

Just for once he could actually do something, save someone. He had been helpless when he was covering the civil war; he could observe, report what was happening, but do nothing useful. That was one reason for the nightmares he had had ever since he got back. He was ridden with guilt.

He had barely spoken to the redhead—what had Sara Ounissi called her? Keira, he thought—unusual name; it suited her.

He had noticed her, though; who could help it? That lovely face, the mane of wild red hair, the grace of her body made her unforgettable.

He jumped down, banged on her front door. 'Keira? Keira, are you there? Open the door.'

There was no reply, just an echoing silence, but he was beginning to have a weird feeling, a gut instinct that there really was something wrong. His instincts had been honed by his job. Constantly being around sudden death made you quicker to pick up on danger.

It didn't always work, of course. Sometimes you got caught out. The villagers he had been with that last night before he was shot were now either dead or homeless. It had been a pretty, white-walled, red-roofed little village with apple blossom on the trees in the gardens when he'd first arrived there. He had been enchanted by it, had thought of it as an oasis of peace in the midst of turmoil.

Perhaps the very arrival of him and his camera team had drawn the enemy's attention to the village. They had only been there a short time before the first shells had hit. Within days it was just a mass of smoking rubble, a hole in the ground, and there had been nothing he could do to stop the destruction, to help the people, except to tell the world what was happening to them, and to do that he had had to risk his own life, and that of his team, by staying with them.

The others had survived intact—the cameraman, the sound man, the young director with them on his first war coverage. Only Gerard had been wounded. He had been got out finally by some British soldiers serving there with the United Nations force, flown back to London by his newspaper, given the best possible treatment. His head wound was healing well. It had been a scalp injury, nothing serious; a bullet had ploughed a path across his head, a bloody parting in his hair. The wound in his leg had left him with a limp, most noticable when he was tired. He had been assured that it would gradually pass off altogether. The injuries to his mind were longer-lasting and made him sensitive to atmosphere.

He was sure he wasn't imagining the sense of disaster he was getting now.

'Keira! Open the door or I'm coming in!' he shouted. The builders who had converted this small cottage had used pretty flimsy materials; he was sure he could kick this door in without trouble.

But he hesitated—maybe he shouldn't risk a physical assault on the door in his present condition? His leg wasn't yet fully recovered. He wouldn't want to undo the work of his doctors.

He could try a little light burglary, though. He had once interviewed a professional criminal who had cheerfully demonstrated his own skill at opening hotel doors with a credit card. Gerard had never yet got around to testing what he had learnt. Now was his chance to do so.

He got out his credit-card wallet, extracted a card; a photograph fell out and he picked it up, frowning down at the image of himself in diving equipment against a background of blue sea and sky. It had been taken on his first visit to the country which, unknown to him, was about to be dragged down into civil war. He had spent several holidays there before the conflict began. Gerard had loved the place, gone diving, lazed in the sun, visited the beauty spots, admired the archaeological sites, drunk the local wine, eaten peasant food, strongly flavoured garlic sausages, fish caught on the day you ate it. He had made friends with local people, picked up something of the language, as he always did wherever he went. He had felt no warning of what was to come so soon afterwards.

It had been a painful shock to go back and find the countryside he remembered as peaceful and sun-drenched being torn apart by civil war, the worst of all wars. He had felt so helpless, so useless, faced with such terrible suffering. He couldn't get over what he had seen; he had had nightmares ever since he got back—had woken up screaming in the hospital ward, fought with his nurses, been half crazy with rage and horror.

That was why he was still on sick leave, although he had been pestering the news editor to put him back in the game. He had been ordered to rest and recover mentally before they sent him abroad again.

They thought he was off his trolley, of course. Damn them! Didn't they realise he needed to bury those memories under a heap of others? He needed to be busy, to have things to do to stop himself remembering.

Impatiently Gerard pushed the photo back into his wallet and turned his attention to the front door; he slid his credit card slowly and carefully into position. He heard a click and gently pushed; the door magically slid open.

'Well, well, aren't you clever?' he said to himself, grinning, before he looked around.

The cottage was an exact replica of his own in terms of structure. The front door opened out into a tiny passage at the base of the stairs. Ahead of

him he saw a kitchen, to his right the open door
of the sitting-room.

'Keira!' he called, walking towards the kitchen
door. Then he stopped, shaken by what he saw. It
had been expensively furnished in high-tech style
with every modern gadget and piece of equipment—
but at the moment it looked as if it had been raided
by vandals. The fridge door hung open, food spilled
out on the floor next to it; there was partly eaten
food on the table, on the tops of the cabinets,
everywhere.

Otherwise, though, the room was empty. The girl
must be upstairs. What sort of state was she in? He
began to run, taking the stairs two at a time.

She wasn't in either of the small bedrooms; both
were feminine, delicately furnished, immaculate.
The excessive neatness of the rooms compared to
the disarray in the kitchen sent a shiver down his
spine.

The bathroom door was shut. He tentatively
turned the handle; the door wasn't locked, but he
didn't like to walk in—first he tapped on it, called
her name again.

'Keira? This is your next-door neighbour, Gerard
Findlay. Are you OK? Your friend Sara is worried
about you. Open the door, Keira.'

There was a faint movement inside, then a low,
smothered groan. It was enough to make Gerard
forget social conventions. He burst into the room,
flinched in shock at what he saw. She lay on the
floor just inside the door, curled in a foetal position. As he stopped beside her she lifted her head
as if it was heavy, turned her wet-lashed green eyes
towards him, made a sound, like a terrified kitten.

'Go away!'

She swallowed visibly; he could see that the convulsive movement hurt, saw her wince. No doubt her throat was raw. She must have been throwing up for a long time. She was as white as paper and her mouth was puffy and looked bruised.

Gerard was essentially a very practical man; his common sense took over.

'Have you stopped vomiting?' he quietly asked.

She closed her eyes, sobbed, put a hand to her mouth to stifle the sound, turning her head away from him as if to shut out the sight of him.

'Go away!' she gasped. 'Please . . . just leave me alone.'

He took no notice. Bending, he lifted her bodily, putting one hand under her knees, another under her back. It was no problem to him—he was a very strong man; his muscles took her weight easily. She was as light as a feather anyway; she seemed to have no bones; he almost believed that if he dropped her she wouldn't fall, she would float.

'No,' she wailed, but he ignored the protest, carrying her through into the bedroom. He lowered her gently on to the bed, sat her on the edge of it, still holding her with one hand while he pulled her thin blue silky tunic dress up over her head with the other.

She tried to fight him off, to stop him. 'What are you doing?' she gasped in panic.

He got the dress off, however, and threw it into a corner of the room. Under it she was wearing a one-piece garment, white silk, the top of it held up by fine thin straps over her bare shoulders, the deep

white lace frothing over her breasts, matching lace
ending at the pale thighs.

'Bastard,' she spat out, the green eyes flashing
as she saw him looking down at her body curiously.
'Get your hands off me. I'm not in such a bad way
that I can't stop you raping me.' Her fingers curled
into claws; she had long, pale, pearl-vanished nails
which looked lethal. 'I'll have your eyes out if you
try it!'

'You must be joking!' snapped Gerard, suddenly
angry with her for what she was doing to herself.
'You don't think any man could find you sexy,
looking like this?'

Her green eyes widened; she gave him a stricken
look.

He grimaced, wishing he hadn't said that. More
gently, he told her, 'I took your dress off because
I thought you'd feel better in something clean.'

She took that on board and flinched as she
realised what he meant. 'Oh, God,' she groaned,
covering her face with her hands. 'What do I look
like? Don't look at me. Go away; please go away.'

He laid her down on the bed and went over to
the wall-to-wall fitted wardrobe. He pulled out a
warm blue wool dressing-gown and brought it back
to her.

She was lying on the bed with closed eyes, curled
into the foetal position again as if wishing to re-
treat back into a time before birth, back to the
safety of the womb. The wild red hair spilled over
the pillow; her skin was like buttermilk; the small
breasts with their dark pink nipples had the bud-
like look of a very young girl's. Her bra was clearly
padded. But those legs... His eyes followed the

graceful length of them down to those thin, high-instepped feet. She was far too thin, but she was hauntingly lovely. A faery child, he thought; not quite of this world.

How old was she? he wondered, guessing her to be not much past twenty. Maybe twenty-one or two? A good ten years younger than himself.

'You'd better put this on,' he told her, and her eyes snapped open. She sat up and he held the dressing-gown for her while she weakly pushed her arms into it; Gerard knelt down to tie the wide blue belt around her tiny waist. She was so fragile it made him almost afraid to touch her, and he grew angry again.

'How can you do such stupid things to yourself?' he asked her, looking up into her face. 'You don't need to diet, you have a beautiful body; why are you trying to destroy it for the sake of vanity?'

'Vanity?' She laughed with a rising edge that made him frown. He didn't think he could cope with female hysteria. 'You think I like myself?' she asked him wildly. 'Don't tell me I have a beautiful body; I know how fat I am. I have eyes; I can see myself in a mirror.'

He looked his amazement, his eyes widening and his jaw dropping. 'Fat? You aren't fat! You can't honestly believe that. If anything, you're too skinny.'

'Don't lie to me! Oh, I know you mean well, but there's no point in pretending. I'm not a fool.'

'You may not be a fool but you're definitely crazy,' said Gerard grimly. 'I'm going to ring your doctor, get you some help.'

'No!' She gripped his arm with fingers that dug into him. 'I won't see him!' Her voice was hoarse but insistent.

Gerard had no idea what to do in this situation; he didn't really know what he was dealing with. Sara Ounissi had been so urgent, so scared. And his first reaction when he'd seen Keira had been one of shock and dismay. Yet now he wasn't sure how serious this was—she was very pale, admittedly, and everything she said disturbed him, yet he didn't get the feeling that this was a silly girl, a butterfly with nothing much in her head. Her green eyes were far too intelligent, her mouth full and warm, yet determined.

He had better wait for Sara to get back; she would know what to do.

As if picking up his thoughts and echoing them, Keira moistened her bruised mouth with the tip of her tongue and said huskily, 'You said... Sara was here? Where...?'

'She went to get a key from the agent; I can't think what's taking her so long. Would you like a glass of water? Or is there any medication you take?'

'Water would be wonderful, please,' she whispered.

There was a sound of running feet on the stairs at that instant and Sara Ounissi appeared in the doorway of the bedroom. She stopped dead, her long black hair tumbled around her white face, and looked at her friend hurriedly.

'Oh, Keira... are you OK?'

Keira's white mouth trembled into a faint smile. 'I'm just fine,' she said, and tried to get up. A second later she fainted. Gerard was just too late to catch her. She lay face down on the floor while he was still leaping to interrupt her fall.

'Call her doctor!' he ordered Sara before he picked Keira up again and put her back on the bed.

Sara didn't argue. She hurried out without a word. Gerard thought wryly, Her husband must be a very happy man; I hope he knows how lucky he is! Why don't I ever meet girls like her? Well, I did meet her, of course, and never tried to get to know her. How was I to know she was perfect wife material? But then I wasn't looking for a wife. I'm still not, in fact.

Marriage was not part of Gerard's game plan.

He turned back to look at the other girl, his brows dark, his eyes smouldering. He was desperately sorry for her, and yet he was affronted by her too. When he thought of the desperate struggle to survive in spite of everything which he had seen in other places it made him deeply angry to think that this stupid girl, with everything to live for, in a safe, sheltered country, was busy trying to kill herself over silly vanity.

What was her family doing, allowing her to get into this state? He glanced around the room as if looking for clues and saw some photographs on a chest by the window. He went over to look hard at them.

One was of Keira and a woman in a bikini who from a distance looked young, not much older than Keira herself—until you looked more closely, and saw that the tanned skin was faintly wrinkled on the neck, and the face too tight. A face-lift? he thought. Was this her mother? Red hair, green eyes, a tall, very slim woman—who else could it be? He saw the same woman in another photo, again with Keira, but a lot of other people gathered around them, in a luxuriously furnished reception-room with marble floors and chandeliers hanging from the ceiling.

This time they were with a much older man—grey-haired, heavily tanned, wearing a tropical lightweight suit in a pale colour. He had his arm around the red-headed woman and was smiling into the camera.

I know him! thought Gerard. The face was very familiar. But he couldn't remember where he had seen it before. He closely examined the room in the photo—people in Britain didn't go in for marble floors in their homes. That usually meant a Mediterranean setting, which fitted with the blue skies you saw through the open French windows, and the sunlight flooding the room, but the furniture had an Arab look to it.

Tangier? Wasn't that where Keira's stepfather was supposed to be at the moment? Perhaps he had a villa there?

There were pictures crowded together on the walls of the room in the photo. He looked closer, curious, and was impressed as he recognised some well-known, contemporary artists. Gerard was something of an expert on twentieth-century art. He had an art degree and had chosen the artists of post Second World War Europe as the subject of his degree thesis.

These paintings could be copies, of course, but somehow he didn't think it likely. The home in which they hung was far too luxurious. If they were

originals, the owner of the villa must either be very
wealthy or knowledgeable enough to pick up young
artists before their work was highly priced.

Why on earth weren't Keira's parents doing
something about her illness? They obviously had
money. Didn't they care what happened to her? Or
didn't they know? Had she managed to keep her
bulimia a secret from them?

Keira stirred a moment later, black lashes flick-
ering against pale cheeks, a little sigh escaping.

He quickly went back to her. 'Just lie still; don't
move again,' Gerard told her quite gently as the
lashes rose and he found himself looking into those
slanting green eyes. His finger and thumb gripped
her wrist, taking her pulse. It was faint and far-
away; her skin felt icy.

'Where's Sara?' she whispered. Her gaze moved
from his downbent face, flicked around the rest of
the room.

'She's gone to call your doctor.'

'No!' She tried to sit up but he pushed her back
against the pillows, holding her shoulders down,
leaning over.

'Be sensible. For God's sake, girl, do you want
to die?'

If it was possible, she turned whiter, her lips
quivering, then she tried to laugh.

'Don't be so melodramatic! Oh, will you stop
interfering? You may think you're trying to help
me but you're only making things ten times worse.'

'You don't know what's best for you,' Gerard
said obstinately.

She gave him a sarcastic look. 'And you do, of
course! You men are all the same. Sara has married

one who treats her like a cross between a doll and a slave. I can't believe she actually seems to enjoy it; I think she's temporarily insane. Well, I'm not letting you run my life for me, so get out of my home and mind your own business.'

He hadn't been able to do anything to stop the death and misery he had seen during the civil war, but he wasn't going to stand aside and let this girl destroy herself without trying to stop her.

'You'll see a doctor if I have to tie you to that bed,' he insisted.

Sara came back into the room with a glass of water. Gerard lifted Keira and she took the glass, sipped some of the water very slowly, as if allowing it to trickle down her sore throat.

'Dr Patel will be here any minute,' Sara told them.

Keira looked at her furiously. 'You shouldn't have rung him. You know what he'll say. He'll only go through the old routine again, trying to persuade me to go into that stupid clinic, and I'm not going, so you will both have wasted your time. The attack's over, OK? I'm fine; I just had a little hiccup, nothing serious.'

'It looked damned serious to me!' exploded Gerard. 'Your kitchen looks like a bomb's hit it! You need help.'

She flinched, gave him that stricken look again, then turned crossly on her friend. 'What's he doing here? You didn't ask him in, did you? Come to that, what are you doing here? Why aren't you back home with Rashid? How did you both get in here?'

'Benny rang me,' Sara said uneasily. 'He was worried about you.'

'Benny!' The green eyes glittered. 'I might have known! Wait till I get hold of him!'

'He cares about you.' Sara looked pleadingly at her. 'So do I, Keira. I'm sorry you lost the contract.'

'I don't want to talk about it!' She threw Gerard a hostile look. 'And you still haven't told me why *he's* here—what on earth possessed you to involve *him*?'

'I couldn't get in, but I knew you were in there; I heard you at one point. I was desperate, Keira; I thought his front door key might fit your door.'

'You can be so daft!' muttered Keira, scowling.

'Sorry,' Sara said softly. 'I was upset. Gerard was very helpful; he suggested I got another key from the agent—that hadn't occurred to me; I was too upset to think properly. Men always seem to be able to think clearly, however upset they get.' She gave Gerard an admiring smile.

Keira snorted. 'Don't butter him up! He'll be purring in a minute.'

'It was clever of him,' Sara said. 'I drove round to the agent's, but when I got back Gerard had already managed to open the door and was up here with you.'

Keira turned her eyes back to Gerard. 'How...?'

'I slipped the lock with a credit card,' he admitted coolly.

She was outraged. 'I could call the police and have you arrested for that! That's burglary.'

'I thought I might be saving your life! Your friend gave me the impression you could be dying.'

A voice called from downstairs and Sara said with relief, 'Dr Patel!' She went out, called, 'Come up, please, Doctor.'

Keira looked coldly at Gerard. 'Thank you for all your help,' she said sarcastically. 'Goodbye. Shut the front door behind you and if you ever burgle my house again I really will call the police, however good an excuse you think up!'

He got up. 'Thanks for the gratitude. Next time you try to kill yourself I'll just let you go ahead, don't worry.'

He passed the doctor on the landing. 'The best of luck; you'll need it, with her,' he told him, and the startled man gave him a stare, then a sudden, amused grin.

'Oh, don't worry, I know what to expect. She is a very stubborn young lady.'

Gerard headed for work ten minutes later, to have his interview with the news editor, but as he drove through heavy traffic he couldn't get her image out of his head—the wild tangle of red curls around that delicate white face, the bud-like breasts and long, long legs. She haunted him for the rest of the day.

CHAPTER TWO

KEIRA was thinking about him too, hardly listening to the doctor as he examined her, sighing.

'You've stopped putting on weight, haven't you? Have you lost some more? You were doing so well, too. You must not let yourself slide backwards, my dear girl.' His sing-song voice was gently sad; he never became angry, he just got sadder and sadder. Trying to make me feel guilty, thought Keira. And succeeding a lot of the time! Dr Patel was a great psychologist.

'It just happened,' was all Keira could say to him. She felt like death, and knew she must look it. She had seen the distaste in Gerard Findlay's eyes and felt sick herself. He was the very last man in the world she would have wanted to see her in that condition. It had been a deep shock to find herself looking into his eyes. For a second she had almost thought she was imagining him, and then she had realised he was not a figment of her imagination, he was really there, and she had been shaken to her depths.

'Just happened?' the doctor repeated, shaking his head in disbelief. 'Oh, please, Keira! We both know there is more to it than that!'

Keira looked at him helplessly, her face white, her eyes smudged and shadowy in that whiteness. 'All right! I couldn't cope. When I knew I'd lost that contract I felt so bad. I didn't mean to let it happen. I came home and I was hungry; I started to eat, and the next minute...'

'It triggered an attack.' Dr Patel nodded. 'It is insidious. Something makes you unhappy, you need the comfort of food, you start to eat and you can't stop, but you are afraid of putting on weight, so you make yourself throw up. It is an endless circle. The only way out of it is understanding yourself and why it happens. As soon as you feel yourself losing control you must stop, go for a walk, go to see a film, ring up friends, visit people, do anything to distract yourself.'

'I know, I know. Oh, and I tried so hard this last year; it hasn't happened for months and months; I kept it under tight control, put on lots of weight.'

'You needed to,' the doctor said quickly, frowning at her. 'Don't start telling yourself you're fat! You know that's another trigger. The truth is, you're still underweight for your height.'

He saw the evasion in her face and knew she didn't really believe him; that was the problem with all bulimia sufferers—they couldn't trust in what they saw in the mirror. They saw a very different reflection and they never believed what other people told them, either. Their obsession was too deep, as deep as their need for love and reassurance.

'Keira, Keira,' he said, shaking his head at her. 'Believe me, you are too thin. My wife is a very sexy woman, most beautiful, and she would make two of you!'

That made her laugh and her face relaxed a little. 'She wouldn't thank you for that if she could hear you!'

Dr Patel's eyes twinkled. 'Oh, she would be flattered—in my culture being thin is not so prized as it is in yours. I like women to have round hips and breasts like watermelons. I don't want to go to bed with someone with the figure of a boy. That doesn't excite me at all.' He grinned at her. 'I am sorry, Keira, but you would have to put on a lot of weight before I would think you were as beautiful as my wife!'

Keira giggled, then said wryly, 'But I'm a model, Doctor. I have to stay slim or I won't get work. The camera puts pounds on you. That's why I lost that Rexel contract—they thought I had put on too much weight.'

He looked irritated. 'Then they are very silly people. You are much more beautiful now than you were a year ago! A little weight has improved you.'

'Tell that to Rexel's ad men,' Keira said bitterly.

The doctor watched her shadowed face and sighed.

'I wish I could have the chance! I would box their ears for them. Believe me, you have been looking much better lately. It is a great pity to ruin it now; you don't want to have to go back to the clinic, do you?'

She shook her head, grimacing, remembering the regime in the private clinic to which her stepfather had sent her when her weight had got down so far that it had shocked her mother when she'd seen Keira again after a gap of eighteen months.

Keira had agreed to have medical help only because her mother was so distraught. Keira hadn't really believed she was ill. The first month in the clinic had been a long struggle between her and the medical staff. It had taken some time before she had begun to listen to them, begun to understand what she had been doing to herself. Since then she had been through a bitter battle to start living a very different life, and she was angry with herself for having fallen back again.

'That's the last thing I want! I couldn't stand going through that again!' she assured the doctor, who smiled.

'Good girl. Then what you must do now is break this pattern before it starts. I think you should take a holiday, get away from the problems that have caused the recurrence.'

'But now I've lost Rexel I'll have to get other work, which means I must be in London.'

'That can wait, my dear, believe me. The most important thing at the moment is for you to get back to the position you were in a year ago, feeling strong and sure of yourself. Going away will help you see things more clearly; from a distance everything will look different. Go somewhere sunny. Just relax and have fun, forget everything else. Eat three meals a day, never eat alone, don't eat in between meals, but above all if you feel an attack threatening do something. Get a friend to go with you, stop you going near food. That little girl out there— Sara, is it? Get her to go with you. And while you're there go out all the time, keep busy, surround yourself with lots of people.' He smiled at her. 'You have broken the cycle once, my dear. Don't let it re-establish itself.'

'I won't. Thank you, Dr Patel.' Keira smiled at him. His soothing manner and understanding had made her feel more human.

When he had gone Sara came into the bedroom and sat on her bed. 'What did he say?'

Keira told her and Sara nodded. 'I think that's very good advice. You haven't had a holiday for ages, you've been working so hard.'

'Rexel kept me busy,' Keira said, her mouth turning down at the corners as she was reminded of the lost contract. She had hoped for so much from it—the constant appearance on TV had been making her face instantly recognisable everywhere she went. Being seen on magazine covers, or inside magazines, never had that sort of impact. Of course, she had known it couldn't last forever, but she had hoped for another year, at least.

Sara gave her a sympathetic look. 'I'm sorry, Keira—it must have been a terrible blow. But at least now you're free to take other work, and after you've been the Rexel girl and on TV all the time for a year your face is famous—you're bound to be offered lots of jobs.'

'For a while, maybe. But I'm getting too old! You know how young you have to be in this business. In a few years the place will be overrun with girls of seventeen who'll get all the jobs, and I'll be out, finished. I'll be lucky to get a job modelling clothes for home-shopping catalogues.'

'You're just depressed. You've got plenty of time to make it into the big league; you're only twenty-two.'

'I feel a lot older.' Keira grimaced, her mouth turning down at the edges, then shot Sara an accusing look. 'By the way, I've got a bone to pick with you.'

'A bone?' For once Sara's brilliant grasp of English failed her; she stared blankly.

'Gerard Findlay!'

'Oh...' Sara put one of her elegant little hands up to her mouth, giggling helplessly.

'It isn't funny! You know I hate the man—I certainly didn't want him to see me looking like that! I could kill you!'

Sara looked apologetically at her. 'Sorry, I was in a panic. I just needed...'

'A man to tell you what to do!' Keira finished for her, eyeing her with half-impatient amusement. 'I know you; when a problem comes up you always scream for a man.'

'They are so useful! I wasn't brought up to break down doors; think what it would do to my nails!'

Keira looked at Sara's long, beautiful manicured fingernails and laughed. Sara was smart, lively, very shrewd and down-to-earth, when she was with her own sex; but let a man walk into the room and she threw a switch, started fluttering her lashes, using a soft, sweet voice, acting dumb and helpless. And the really maddening thing, thought Keira, was that it always seemed to work; men loved it. Had Gerard Findlay liked it?

Sara added triumphantly, 'And I was right: he got in here, didn't he? And without having to break the door down. He is clever...' She grinned. 'As well as very sexy.'

Keira wished she could deny it, but much as she might dislike Gerard Findlay she couldn't ignore his smouldering sexuality. The first time she'd seen him he had made an indelible impact with his black hair and angry grey eyes, that lean and powerful body. He was intensely male, and he made Keira deeply aware of her own sexuality. Everything female in her vibrated in response, as if buried deep inside her was a magnetic needle which quivered and swung towards the north pole of his masculinity.

'I hate the man,' she repeated, and Sara gave her a glinting, teasing smile.

'That's what *you* say.'

To her own fury, Keira felt her skin colour, glow hot. At that second the telephone rang. Deeply relieved to be able to change the subject, she said, 'Could you answer that? Ask whoever it is to leave a name and number and I'll call them back later.'

'OK,' Sara said, then, with a mocking flick of her lashes added, 'Saved by the bell!'

Keira did not ask her what she meant. Sara was intensely intuitive, unfortunately. She picked up feelings and thoughts Keira did not want her to guess at; it was part of Sara's strongly developed femininity, which was half instinctive, half learnt at her mother's knee.

It was the merest accident that Sara came to be in London, let alone working as a model. Her Arab parents had brought her to London when she was four because her father got a job with an Arab bank in Mayfair. When Sara was six, he had died, and her ravishing, still very young mother had stayed on in London because her brother worked in the same bank and was at hand to take care of his sister and her child.

Sara's mother was young and beautiful; within a year she had married again, a client of the bank with an enormous fortune. Sara had lived in

England ever since. At seventeen she had become a model and had been very successful. Her family made sure she never took her clothes off in front of a man, never modelled underclothes or swimwear, but that had not hindered her career. She had begun by working with one of her cousins, a talented young designer who modelled his clothes on her: Arab-inspired caftans and evening dresses, hooded cloaks that swirled around you as you walked, filmy loose white gauze trousers tied at the ankles. His clothes were romantic, visually exciting; he had helped make Sara's reputation, she had begun to appear on magazine covers and was soon in great demand. When she'd retired from the profession to get married, aged twenty-one, a wail of regrets had gone up from the photographers and designers who liked to have her work for them.

Sara had been blithely indifferent. Oh, she had enjoyed modelling, but now she was eager to be a wife and mother. Sara always threw herself whole-heartedly into whatever she was doing, and loved variety, excitement, novelty—she got bored doing the same thing every day. What she wanted was constant change.

Keira frowned at the ceiling, her face as cold and white as the plasterwork above her. I wish I did, she thought, but change of any kind, in her work, in her private life, made her tense and nervous and there was nothing she could do to stop that knee-jerk reaction.

While she was staying at the clinic she had undergone therapy which tried to get at the root of her eating disorder and made her aware that the various problems she had all stemmed from the same source, her childhood and the breakdown of the family which had changed her world forever at exactly the worst age, on the verge of puberty. It was one thing to realise something like that, quite another to be able to deal with it. You could re-train yourself where learned behaviour was concerned, but when you were dealing with the unconscious you could not use reason or persuasion; you were helpless to reach that submerged part of the mind.

She started, hearing Sara's running feet on the stairs. The other girl came back into the room, flushed and smiling. 'It was your mother.'

Keira tensed. 'You didn't tell her I'd had an attack?'

'No. Although I know I ought to have—she'll be furious when she knows I didn't tell her.'

'She'll tell Ivo, and he'll just use it as a stick to beat her with!'

Sara gave her a curious look. 'You hate him, don't you?'

'He isn't my man of the year, I'll admit.'

'Well, I told your mother you were out and would ring her back when you got in; don't forget to do that when you feel up to it.' She looked at her watch. 'I'll have to go; we're having a dinner party tonight. I'll ring you later to check how you are. If you need me, you know where I am.'

'Yes,' Keira said, then added quietly, 'Thanks, Sara—for coming so quickly and...' She made a wordless little gesture with her hands and Sara shook her head at her.

'What are friends for? Be seeing you soon.'

*   *   *

In the newsroom of the TV company he worked for Gerard was arguing with the news editor, a large, shaggy-haired man with heavy eyebrows and a permanently harassed look.

'I tell you there's nothing wrong with me now; I'm as fit as you are.' He gave the other man a furious look from head to toe, scowling. 'Fitter, come to that!'

The other man, who was stones overweight, drank like a fish and smoked like a chimney, laughed.

'Sure, you are, but I'm not a foreign correspondent, I'm a desk jockey, and I don't need a doctor's certificate before I come to work. I have to abide by the company doctor's decision and he says you shouldn't be sent into a war zone again, or put under any strain, because you're still suffering from...' He searched among the piled papers on his desk and pulled out one, pushed his spectacles up on his forehead and peered at the document. 'Here it is...post-traumatic shock. That's what you've got, Gerry, old son. You're in post-traumatic shock and the company won't be responsible for you if you go abroad. They don't want to have to pay out huge sums of money in compensation if you crack up permanently next time.'

'Damn fools!' growled Gerard, but recognised that he had no hope of persuading the company to change their mind. Money was the bottom line with these people.

'Listen, didn't you do an art degree? Todd's on to an interesting art story—it may develop into a full programme for current affairs, or just turn out to be a stock item for one of those nights when there's no news. He could do with some help; why not work with him for a week and then have another check-up?'

Gerard gave a furious shrug. 'Oh, very well. Where will I find him?'

'He's working out of Annexe Three—you'll need a pass; security is pretty tight at the moment. Hang on; I'll ring him and warn him you're on your way and he'll alert Security.'

Todd Knight was a short, ginger-haired man in his early thirties; he was the news team's art and antiques expert but doubled up by reporting on certain crime stories when they touched on his specialist subject.

He welcomed Gerard with open arms. 'Good to have you aboard, man! I could do with some help with this stuff; I'm absolutely swamped with leads and I can't follow them all up personally. You're a godsend.'

Gerard grinned at him, accepting the mug of black coffee Todd offered him. 'Glad to be of some use for a change. So, what's it all about?'

'The underground trade in stolen art and antiques.' Todd gestured to the walls of the office on which hung photographs and drawings. 'All these disappeared during the past two years. They're important works, most of them—worth millions. None of them resurfaced, so where are they? Who took them, and who bought them from the thieves?'

Gerard frowned, wandering around the room, peering at the snapshots. 'This is police work, surely—they have a squad which specialises in following up these cases.'

'Of course they do, and they are, but I'm working on an idea for a programme; I believe international collectors are involved in a crime ring, employing criminals who are given exact orders—told what to snatch and how much will be paid when the painting is delivered. It's being organised on a huge scale, Gerard, and it's a worldwide scam.'

Gerard whistled. 'That could make some programme! Hey, I know this painting…it was hanging in a gallery in the South of France; it's a Cézanne.'

'Right—it vanished a year ago, hasn't been seen since. There's a strong lead over in France, in Provence; I was thinking of going over there soon to see what I can dig up.'

'You can count me in for that—a few days in Provence sounds great; I think I'm going to enjoy this job!' grinned Gerard. 'Oddly enough, I was going to ring you today anyway—I wanted to ask you a few questions.'

Keira half slept, half daydreamed for several hours and then got up and showered, got dressed. It was twilight by then, early evening. She forced herself to think about supper, and decided to have a little scrambled egg, followed by a banana. Her stomach still felt queasy but she knew she had to re-establish a light eating pattern at once.

She went downstairs, almost jumping out of her skin when her doorbell rang loudly just as she reached the tiny hallway.

She hesitated, but she couldn't pretend not to be in because she had only just switched on the hall light.

'Who is it?' she asked, close to the door.

'Gerard Findlay,' said the deep, familiar voice, and she closed her eyes. It would be him, wouldn't it?

'What do you want?'

'To talk to you. Open this door; I don't like talking through it with half the street listening. Of course, if you don't mind everyone hearing what I say to you...' He paused significantly, and she bit her lip, flushed with anger. He knew very well that she wouldn't want anyone eavesdropping, especially if he meant to talk about what had happened earlier that day.

Reluctantly, she slipped the catch and opened the door, very tense as she faced him. He looked her up and down with those hard grey eyes, taking in everything about her, from her faintly damp red hair, tied up with a black ribbon at her nape, down over her slender figure to her pale bare feet. She had not bothered to put on make-up and was wearing a black sweater and jeans. She looked, thought Gerard, like a boy, and yet there was something so intensely feminine about her mouth, naturally full and pink, as velvety as a hedgerow rose, so that he couldn't help wondering what it would taste like, how it would feel if he kissed it. His gaze wandered to that wild, tumbling hair; she had tried to tame it by tying it back but it suited her better free—he was tempted to catch hold of it, pull off the ribbon and let the hair fall around her face, before running his fingers through it, burying his face in the curling strands.

Keira stared back at him angrily—how dared he look her over like that?

'Well?' she demanded, her chin lifted in a defiant movement.

'Feeling better?' he asked casually.

She nodded without a smile, her expression offhand, which, if he had known her better, he would have known meant that she was ill at ease and desperately trying to hide it.

'I'm fine. You said you had something to say. Could you be quick? I'm very busy.'

His lids half lowered at that, a sardonic gleam in his eyes as he surveyed her.

'Going out?'

She hesitated. 'I might.'

'Dressed like that?' His glance ran over her again with open amusement, but underneath that he was reacting very differently. He kept telling himself she was too skinny for his taste, but the truth was he found those small, high breasts sexy, even though the baggy sweater half hid her body—the body he had been remembering all day, the body he had carried in his arms and found as light as a child's yet with considerable sensual impact.

'I shall change if I go out,' she coldly told him. 'You still haven't told me what you wanted to say.'

He shrugged. 'I just wanted to check you were OK.'

'I'm fine, thank you, as I just told you.' Her tone was curt, rejecting his interest.

He was undeterred; Gerard Findlay had spent his entire working life persisting in the face of angry resistance to his questioning. 'What did the doctor say?'

She gave him a furious look at that, green eyes sparking fire. 'Why on earth should I tell you that?

I know you're a reporter but that doesn't give you the right to go around asking people about their private lives! If I told you I might find the story in a gossip column tomorrow!'

'I'm a foreign correspondent on TV, not a gossip columnist with a tabloid!' he retorted. 'And I've no intention of selling your story to either the newspapers or TV. I saw your light on as I was parking my car, so I thought I'd check that you were OK. I wish I hadn't bothered now.'

He turned on his heel and went out, banging the door behind him with a violence that made her nerves shiver. She knew she had been rude and hostile and he had only been showing neighbourly concern, she knew she ought to go after him to apologise but she couldn't. She had to keep him at arm's length. She had known that from the minute she first saw him.

She remembered that afternoon with crystal-clarity. It had been a cool November Saturday, the last bronze leaves blowing off the trees and rustling in the gutters, the sky almost entirely colourless.

Because it was the weekend neither she nor Sara had been working. Normally they did their housework and shopping on a Saturday, and they had just finished tidying the cottage when the removal van had arrived next door.

'This must be our new neighbour,' Sara had said, leaning out of the window to watch the arrival. The cottage next door had been empty for several weeks and they had known that a new tenant would shortly be taking over.

The van had parked, the removal men had climbed down and undone the tailboard, at which point Gerard had arrived, roaring up at speed in his little red sports car.

'Nice car!' Sara commented approvingly, then whistled as the driver got out to unlock the front door of the cottage so that the men could carry his furniture inside.

'Look at those long legs; I do love men with long, long legs.'

'You love men, full stop,' Keira told her drily.

'True.' Sara curled up on the window-seat, like a curious little cat, to watch everything that was going on next door. 'I'm sure I know him. I've seen him before somewhere, I just can't remember where.'

Keira went off to make coffee for them both. When she got back Sara told her excitedly, 'I've got it! He's on the news, on TV...not an announcer, a reporter—oh, you know, he was on the other night doing a story from Jordan. He must have just flown home. I'm trying to remember his name...Jeremy? Geoffrey?'

'Gerard,' said Keira who had recognised him at once. 'Gerard Findlay.'

'That's it! I knew I was close.' Sara stared in fascination as he moved about below in the mews, that lean, powerful body, in jeans and a leather jacket, as graceful as a wild animal's, a big cat, a leopard or a jaguar. There was that aura of danger about him, the threat of the predator.

'He is simply gorgeous, isn't he?' Sara sighed. 'If I wasn't madly in love with Rashid I would flip over him.'

Keira didn't say anything. She was too busy feeling sick. Her skin was prickling, her stomach clenching; even the hairs on her head had seemed to react to the man moving about between the cottage next door and the street.

She had always liked him on TV, but in real life he was far sexier. The small screen diminished him. When you saw him crouching down behind ruined houses, or talking against a background of such devastation that it overwhelmed the man doing the commentary, you didn't realise how tall he was, how powerfully built. He was more intensely coloured too, his hair a midnight-black, with the sheen of a raven's wing, his skin tanned to a smooth gold, his eyes a dark, glittering grey. Staring at him that first morning, she felt an attraction so strong she was terrified.

She had been in love only once before; she never wanted to feel like that again. She had fallen too hard, become desperate with love; he had been frightened off. She had known it was happening but been unable to stop the need welling up inside her, or even hide it. All her life she had been looking for love, and she'd thought she had finally found it, but she had picked the wrong man to love that much. He had not been an all-or-nothing type. He'd found her need alarming. He'd stopped asking her out and started dating someone else; Keira had gone through a hell of pain and humiliation, because everyone knew, all their friends, and she had been so distressed that she hadn't done a very good job of hiding how she felt.

Two years had gone by since it happened, but it still had the power to sting her when she remembered it.

If she ever fell in love again she was going to do so slowly, and let the man fall in love first, make sure she was safe before she let herself care.

'Let's go round and invite him in for a cup of tea,' Sara said.

Keira shook her head and said, 'You would have to invite all those removal men too, and I'm not in the mood to talk to a lot of strangers.'

'You're crazy,' Sara said, but in the end she took a tray of tea and hastily made sandwiches next door, and came back after being there for ages, laughing and pink, well pleased with herself. She had found out all she could about Gerard, no doubt asked endless questions.

'He's not married, not even divorced; he just broke up with his latest girlfriend . . .'

'I don't care; stop talking about him!'

'I took a lot of trouble checking him out for you!' teased Sara, her eyes dancing. 'He's your type, more so than mine.'

Keira reacted furiously, giving her a glare. 'I don't want any of your matchmaking. If I want a man I'll find my own.'

But Sara persisted in trying to bring them together. 'You'll change your mind when you meet him,' she said, and went round to invite him to their next party. Keira fought to stay indifferent, but by the time the party began she was in a very hyper state. She kept busy pouring drinks, handing around food, but she looked round every time someone arrived, her heart skipping a beat.

Gerard did not come. The hours went by, the party grew louder and louder, neighbours came to complain and usually stayed on for the rest of the party, but there was no sign of the man next door.

When everyone had gone in the early hours, Keira went to bed depressed and angry, as much with herself as with him. She hadn't even met him yet and already she was experiencing those familiar highs and lows which she vividly remembered from two years ago. She didn't want to go through all that again.

From then on Keira ignored him if she passed him on the street, if they happened to leave or arrive back home at the same time.

Sara, though, went on trying to make friends with him for a while—she invited him to another party, but he didn't come to that either. She went round to borrow some milk from him once, on a Sunday, and found his little cottage full of people, friends from the TV company who had come back to his place for breakfast after a party elsewhere. Sara stayed for an hour, and came back hoping she had finally made a breakthrough with him.

But even Sara turned against him when he started complaining about the noise they made. He banged on the wall when Sara was playing her favourite pop music, came round to shout at them to keep the noise down, rang up to complain the next time they had a party which went on all night, and finally complained to the agent, who informed Keira's stepfather, who, in turn, complained to Keira in an icy letter which threatened to turn her and Sara out of the cottage if there were any more complaints.

'He'd do it, too,' Keira told her friend. 'He'd jump at the chance. Ivo has always hated me, because I look like my father, and Ivo is still jealous of him, even though it's years since the divorce.'

'You never see your father either,' Sara thought aloud, not noticing the shadow that passed over Keira's face.

'He hasn't been back from Brazil for six years,' Keira said flatly.

'You should visit him.'

Keira had never been invited to, but she didn't tell Sara that. Instead she marched to the door.

'I'm going round to tell Gerard Findlay what I think of him!' Fuelled by rage, she was sure she could face him at last, but when she got round there and rang the doorbell, knocked loudly on the front door, nobody answered. The place was empty.

He had probably been abroad again. She hadn't seen him, in fact, for weeks, and during that time Sara had got married and moved out, and Keira had been left alone in the cottage. At least there had been no more complaints and so Ivo's threats had stopped, too, to her mother's great relief.

Elise hated any sort of rows; she liked her life peaceful and comfortable. She was not an emotional woman, although she used the language of affection, calling everyone dear and darling, kissing everyone fondly on meeting and parting. She was a beautiful woman, even now, in her late forties. She still turned heads everywhere she went, and Ivo had plenty of excuses for making jealous rows. Elise had never loved him, in Keira's opinion—how could she? He was so much older. How could she have left Keira's father for him?

I suppose I'd better ring her, Keira thought reluctantly. Frowning, she went to the phone and rang

Tangier. There was a delay on the line, so she made her supper, one scrambled egg, a thin slice of toast. Her stomach felt raw; she swallowed down a desire to throw up again, walked around the kitchen tidying up and washing her plate and cup, her knife and fork, the saucepan in which she had scrambled the egg.

She talked to her mother half an hour later. 'How are you, darling?' Elise asked her. She had told Keira not to call her Mummy years ago—just after the divorce. She preferred her daughter to use her first name; she had begun to lie about her age and didn't want a grown-up daughter calling her Mummy in front of men, reminding them that she was a lot older than she looked.

'Fine,' lied Keira.

'That's good. Ivo and I are off to Florida tomorrow for a month so I thought I'd ring and have a chat before we leave.'

'I was thinking of going away myself; I need a holiday. I'm hoping Sara can get away to keep me company.'

'Time you found a man, darling. Girl who looks like you—must be plenty of men after you.'

Keira's teeth met; she didn't answer.

Elise said, 'Is Sara expecting yet? She wants one right away, doesn't she?'

'It's early days; she only got married a few weeks ago; give her time!'

'Poor her when she does. Absolutely foul, having babies—why do you think I never had any more?'

Keira didn't bother to answer that. She knew only too well that her arrival had been a great inconvenience to her mother. Elise had hated being pregnant, had been bored by having a baby, had insisted on having a nanny right away and handing the baby over to her.

'So, where are you going for your hols, darling?' Elise asked.

'I don't know yet. Maybe Italy?'

'That would be gorgeous, but why not come here, darling? Simply marvellous in May, not too hot, and not too many tourists around. You can house-sit the villa for us. The servants will be here to look after you; you and Sara could have a ball.'

Keira didn't hesitate. The villa was luxurious, set in the most ravishing gardens, there were great beaches within easy reach and the town of Tangier was fascinating. Keira wouldn't have gone if Ivo had been there—the two of them hadn't hit it off, and there were always quarrels and scenes when they were together. But with him away the place was irresistible.

'Thank you, that would be wonderful—but I'm not sure yet if Sara could come and I wouldn't want to be in that house on my own.'

'Well, you're right; it isn't wise for a girl to go around an Arab country on her own, darling, but I'm sure Alima and Hassan would take good care of you! I'd trust them with my life. We'll be here until tomorrow morning. Give me a call if you are able to come here, and I'll let the servants know you'll be arriving. I must rush now; I have masses to do. We leave first thing in the morning.'

'Enjoy yourself.'

'Same to you, darling.' Elise Krensky blew her a kiss and hung up.

Keira rang Sara who exclaimed excitedly then rushed off to talk to Rashid before coming back to the phone in a slightly more subdued mood.

'Darling, Rashid says I can only go for a week— I'm sorry, but he says he can't spare me for any longer than that. Do you still want to go?'

'Of course I do. A week can be a long time,' said Keira. 'I'll ring my mother and let her know—shall we say we'll arrive next Saturday?'

'That's fine by me.'

'I'll book our flights and let you know the details as soon as possible.'

She rang her mother back at once and Elise promised to let the servants in charge of the house know that she and Sara were arriving the following Saturday.

'Use any rooms you want to—except Ivo's, of course; he hates anyone touching anything in his suite. You won't forget that, will you, darling?' Since Keira had grown up her mother had always treated her like a friend; it was a relationship she felt more comfortable with than that of mother-daughter. Sometimes Keira thought Elise would have been much happier if she had been born by a test-tube and brought up by robots.

'We won't go near his suite,' Keira promised.

There was a travel agent just around the corner from the mews. Keira walked round there to book the flights the following afternoon. It had rained in the morning and the pavements were still wet; the air was full of the heavy scent of rain-washed lilac from the gardens behind the mews. Traffic roared along the Embankment, the Thames was grey and calm, a string of barges moving slowly downriver under the bridges.

She had no trouble booking their flights for the Saturday, and walked slowly back with a newspaper under one arm and a basket of fruit and vegetables dangling from the other. The afternoon was growing warmer; there were bees humming among the climbing roses around one of the cottage doors.

As she put her key in her front door she heard a muffled sound in the cottage and froze, her nerves jumping. What was that? One of the mews cottages had been burgled some weeks ago; was this her turn? She pushed the door open, ready to run, and found herself staring straight at Gerard Findlay.

For a second neither of them moved or spoke, then the spell broke and Keira yelled at him, 'What the hell are you doing in my house?'

He visibly hesitated—she saw his grey eyes flicker—before drawling, 'Waiting for you. I came round to check you were OK and got no answer. I was afraid you might be ill upstairs so I let myself in again.'

'I told you never to do that again! How dare you keep breaking into my house? This time I'm calling the police!'

She pushed past him, heading for the phone, and he caught her arm. Flushed and furious, she glared up at him, trying to free herself.

'Get your hands off me!'

She was wearing a dark green glazed cotton dress which cinched her waist tightly and flowed down over her hips, leaving a lot of her long legs bare. On her dark red hair she wore a cream straw boater with a matching dark green ribbon which floated down her back. The effect was summery and elegant, but as they struggled her hat came off and her red hair tumbled down around her face.

Gerard stared down at her, a glitter in his grey eyes. Keira stared back, felt the hair on the back of her neck prickle with awareness of him. The moment stilled; she was scarcely breathing. Gerard's fingers tightened round her arm; he jerked her towards him and she was so taken off guard that she couldn't stop herself. She fell against him, instinctively reaching out to catch hold of his body to stop her fall, her hands splayed against his chest, the silky white shirt under her fingers warm with his body.

The contact sent waves of sensual reaction crashing round her body. She looked up into his face, her green eyes enormous, dilated. Gerard was staring at her mouth. She trembled at the way he was looking at it. Hunger flared inside her. She looked from his eyes to his mouth, watching it come nearer, the hard line of it intensely male. Her lips parted, she was breathing rapidly now, her eyes already half closing long before their mouths met.

His mouth was cool for a second and then hot, sensually demanding. His other hand caught and held the back of her head, holding it captive so that she couldn't pull away even if she wanted to, and Keira did not want to; she was too occupied in kissing him back, her mouth moving fiercely and heatedly under his.

A shudder of pleasure went through her as the kiss deepened; she clutched his shirt, her body swaying, trembling. She had known the instant she set eyes on him outside in the mews the day he'd

moved in next door that she could feel this way
about him, and it had terrified her—it terrified her
now, this heat growing inside her, the sweetness and
pain twisting like a knife in her melting flesh.

Gerard groaned and lifted his head, his lips apart,
dragging air into his lungs in fierce gasps.

He had let go of her. Keira staggered back from
him and reeled against the wall, her hand to her
bruised, hot mouth. She was afraid of how he
would look at her, afraid that he was going to despise her, or be impatient of the need he must have
sensed in the way she'd responded to him. She
should have fought him off, refused to let him kiss
her. She shouldn't have given in so easily, and she
certainly shouldn't have kissed him back with all
her hunger for love in her lips.

She closed her eyes. She couldn't bear to see his
face.

'Get out,' she muttered.

He went without a word; the front door slammed
and she started violently as if he had hit her. Her
nerves were in a terrible state.

White-faced now, she stumbled up the stairs,
thinking, Thank heavens I'm going away for a little
while. Maybe, with luck, he'll have been sent
abroad again by the time I get back from Tangier.
Maybe he'll stay away; maybe I'll have time to get
over him.

She lay down on her bed because her head was
going round and round, as if she had vertigo. Tears
were trickling down her face. It was half an hour
before she had recovered enough to get up and wash
her tear-stained face, brush her tangled hair.

It was not until she went to bed hours later that she discovered that one of the photographs on her chest of drawers had vanished.

Keira frowned over the gap in the row of framed photos. Which one had gone? It took her some time to remember—the missing one was of her, her mother and Ivo in Ivo's suite, at a party, at their villa in Tangier.

Had Gerard taken it? But why on earth should he? What interest could he possibly have in her family?

CHAPTER THREE

KEIRA paced to and fro, anxiously consulting her watch. Sara was late; they should have checked in their baggage by now and got their boarding cards. Had she been held up by traffic on the way to Heathrow?

She suddenly heard her name booming through the terminal. 'Please come to the information desk on the departure floor. Miss Keira Paxton, please...'

An accident! thought Keira, hurrying towards the information desk, pushing her trolley in front of her. Sara has been in an accident. She's been hurt, she's dying, she's dead...

Calm down, she thought, pushing away the panicky thoughts crashing through her head. Wait until you hear the message before you start imagining the worst.

She stopped in front of the desk, smiled at the man behind it, and said, huskily, 'Hello, I'm Keira Paxton—is there a message for me?'

He looked up politely. 'Miss Paxton? Could I see your ticket, please?'

Keira blankly handed him her flight ticket and he scanned it rapidly, then handed it back to her. 'Thank you. We just had a phone message from a Mr Rashid Ounissi. His wife cannot join you on the flight today—she is unwell—some sort of tummy upset, I gathered. But she will be joining you in a few days, when she has recovered. He said you were to go ahead, and ring them when you arrived safely.'

Keira stared at him, her brows knit. What on earth was she to do? Should she go? Or should she try to cancel her own ticket and re-book later when Sara was better? She looked at her watch and saw that she only had fifteen minutes in which to make up her mind. If she didn't book in her luggage soon it would be too late, she would miss the flight anyway, and she wouldn't get a refund on her ticket.

After all, she was here, she had been waiting for an hour—it seemed stupid not to go. But did she want to go there alone?

There would be servants in the villa; a cook, a housekeeper and a gardener all worked there full time and lived in quarters above the double garage on one side of the villa. Their presence was comforting, but Keira would still be sleeping alone in the villa at night, and she wasn't very happy about that. Perhaps she could ask the housekeeper to sleep in the house until Sara arrived?

She glanced towards the sliding glass doors of the airport. Outside it was raining; the sky was grey and the weather seemed set for the day. It was too depressing to contemplate going back to the mews in this weather when she could be sure of hot sunshine in Tangier.

Keira made up her mind. She rushed off towards the check-in desk, handed over her luggage and collected a boarding card. Once that was done she made her way through Customs and Passport Control, and had time to ring Sara's house before her flight was called.

Rashid answered. 'Oh, Keira—you got our message?' To her surprise he sounded euphoric rather than worried. 'I am sorry you are disappointed. Sara is very disappointed too, but our doctor thinks she should not travel for a couple of days. He wants to run a few tests on her——'

'What's wrong?' interrupted Keira anxiously and was startled to hear him chuckle.

'Nothing, nothing, but...' He paused, then said proudly, 'She was ill in the night; we thought it was gastric flu so we called the doctor first thing this morning, and he told us that she is going to have a baby!'

Keira relaxed, smiling widely. 'Oh, that's wonderful, Rashid. I'm so happy for you; I know how much she wants a baby, how much you both do!'

She heard the Tannoy announcing the departure of her flight while Rashid was happily chattering away, and had to stop him.

'I'm sorry, Rashid, my flight was just called; I'll have to go. Give Sara my love; tell her I'll be in touch and if she doesn't feel up to it she isn't to think of coming over to Tangier.'

Rashid promised to give Sara the message. 'She's in bed resting at the moment but I know she really wants to come—perhaps we'll both fly over; would that be possible, for me to join you both?'

'Of course! You'd be very welcome,' she said, and then had to ring off.

It took two hours to fly to Tangier from London and, having nobody to talk to, Keira was left alone with her thoughts. Staring out at the white cloud layer, the blue and gold of the morning which showed through it, she drifted in and out of daydreams in which Gerard Findlay kept appearing. Each time she realised what she was thinking about she banished him angrily, but he kept coming back.

She hadn't seen him since the hot afternoon when he had kissed her; she had relived those moments over and over again, waking and sleeping. The man wouldn't go away. I hope by the time I get back he'll have been sent abroad again! she thought as the plane landed.

Emerging into vivid sunshine, Keira was met by her stepfather's gardener who also doubled as a chauffeur when required. His grey-striped djellabah made him look taller and thinner than ever, he wore a skull-cap on his black hair, his skin was pock-marked from a brush with smallpox years ago, and he had liquid dark eyes and a warm smile. His wife, Yasmin, small and anonymous in her black robes, her face half veiled, stood beside him.

'Hello, Hassan, hello, Yasmin,' Keira began, delighted to see their familiar faces, then remembered a few words of greeting in Arabic.

Yasmin bobbed her veiled head, answering in Arabic; Hassan spoke in English. 'Welcome back to Morocco, Miss Keira. Please, let me take your luggage.' He relieved her of the suitcase and overnight bag which she was carrying. 'You have a friend with you, yes? We wait for her?'

'No, she couldn't come today; she'll be coming later.'

He looked dismayed. 'You came alone?' Hassan had learnt his English when he'd worked for an American diplomat, and had a strong American accent. Muslims avoided speaking to, touching or being alone with a woman who was not of their

family, but Hassan had worked for Keira's stepfather for years, and had known Keira as a child;
he regarded her as a member of his extended family,
and, no doubt, although he would not tell her so,
as she had no husband to take care of her, saw
himself as standing in for her father.

'I only found out that my friend was not coming
when she didn't turn up at the airport,' explained
Keira.

Why did she feel she had to apologise for that?
she thought wryly, but as she looked into Hassan's
worried eyes she saw that he took her arrival alone
very seriously and could foresee problems. She had
realised it would cause trouble; in an Arab country
it was not wise for a woman to travel alone, however
short the distance.

His wife murmured something to him and Hassan
looked at her, nodding, answered in Arabic, then
turned to Keira and said softly, 'We will make ar-
rangements! Come, my car is in the car park—it is
not far!'

She followed him and felt the heat of the sun
strike her like a blow as they emerged into the light.
Around her bustled men and women in European
dress, queuing to get into a waiting coach, Arab
men in djellabahs of various colours, white, grey,
striped, dark brown, Arab women in black, veiled,
heads bent as they shepherded their children.

Tangier was a city where yesterday and tomorrow met; there was a dramatic contrast between the walled kasbah quarter, built centuries ago,
on a hill above the sea, with its narrow, winding
passages over cobbles, its dark little shops and
minarets, and the busy modern town of white-

washed concrete apartment blocks, set among palms and cypress and green lawns, with the blue of swimming-pools showing here and there.

The Tangier peninsula jutted out from the rest of the Moroccan coastline, which here was separated from Europe merely by a narrow strait of water on the other side of which lay Gibraltar and Spain. The Jebel Mousa, the high land dominating the Moroccan side, and the rocky heights of Gibraltar, on the other, were known to the ancient world as The Pillars of Hercules, the western gateway to the Mediterranean.

Ivo Krensky's villa lay in an expensive residential district on the outskirts of Tangier, on high ground with a distant view of the sea. Before they reached it, they drove through olive and orange groves, and rough countryside where sheep grazed and a flock of goats scrambled, followed by their young shepherd, a thin boy in a loose garment of unbleached cotton. Even here, though, one could not forget that this was a desert country; in the far distance lay a pale glimmer of desert and beyond that in the clear, dry air you could glimpse the sand-coloured peaks of the Atlas mountains.

Keira sat in the back of the car with Hassan's wife beside her; Yasmin was too shy to speak much, answering Keira with little nods, her eyes smiling over her veil, sometimes murmuring very softly, 'Yes...' to show that she had understood something Keira had said.

It did not take long, though, to reach the house, which was set among green gardens behind high white walls. The gates were electronically controlled; Hassan operated them from the car, and they swung open, closing behind the car as it swept away up the wide drive, which was bordered on both sides by palm trees.

Smooth green billiard-table lawns lay behind the trees; set among them were rose beds, banks of bougainvillaea, and there were swags of strawberry-pink clematis clambering over the high white walls around the estate. The car stopped outside the house and Hassan came round to open the door for her. Keira got out, staring at the deep blue of the sky, the white walls and green tiles of the house.

At the massive studded front door of the house stood Alima, the housekeeper, a half-veil covering the lower part of her face and her dark eyes smiling over it.

Walking towards her, Keira felt that she had travelled through more than space since she'd left London. Here she moved in another culture, had to remember what she had learnt on previous visits—that one had to bear constantly in mind the sensitivities of the people here, and try to think in a different way if one was not to cause offence.

'Hello, Alima—how are you?' Keira said, breaking into a smile and offering her hand.

'I am very well; I hope you are, Miss Keira?' Alima was Hassan's sister, a woman in her late forties, a widow with two sons to educate, both of whom were at university in Rabat, one studying law and the other chemistry.

Hassan's wife, Yasmin, did all the cooking, and one of his sons was already beginning to work in the garden with his father, so the villa was run entirely by the family, who, when the owner and his wife were away, were left in sole control of the estate.

The villa was not so much a home as a palace— Ivo Krensky was a very wealthy man although Keira had never been quite sure how he had made his money. He had been born in Russia around sixty years ago, had somehow made his way to America, and was now retired. He spent a great deal of money on his wife, on their home, and on his collection of paintings and antiques, the cream of which was concentrated in his private suite, although there were lovely, precious things scattered throughout the villa.

The geometric-tiled marble-floored hall ended in graceful white pillars supporting the flowing Moorish arches which led into spacious reception-rooms. A small stone bowl in which green fern and rushes grew took up the centre of the hall; from within the plants rose a small fountain which kept up a soothing splash of water while they talked. Keira had forgotten until now, when she suddenly remembered sitting on the low stone wall on hot summer days listening to that noise with bliss.

Hassan spoke to his sister while his wife was vanishing towards the kitchen quarters, then he carried the luggage upstairs while Keira and Alima followed.

'Your mother said you were to choose whichever bedroom you liked, except, of course, the master's suite, which is always kept locked when he is away,' said Alima.

'I'm happy with the room I had last time.'

'It is a pretty room,' smiled Alima.

Hassan had heard her; he went into a large room looking over the gardens, placed the luggage on a chest by the end of the bed and went over to open the shutters, to let the afternoon sunshine into the room, which had been shadowy and cool.

'Your friend has not come, my brother tells me,' Alima said quietly. 'Hassan does not think you should sleep in the villa alone. We have never been burgled—there is a security system operating around the estate—but you never know. I could sleep here until your friend arrives.'

Keira smiled with relief. 'I'd feel easier if you did.'

'Of course you would!' nodded Alima. 'I am happy to.'

Hassan had listened; he smilingly bowed. 'Is there anything else I can do for you, Miss Keira?'

She shook her head. 'No, thank you, Hassan. I am very grateful for being so well looked after.'

'It is nothing,' he assured her.

When he had gone Keira asked Alima politely, 'How are your sons, Alima? Doing well at university?'

Alima's face lit up. 'Oh, yes, they are good boys. I visit them at Rabat once or twice a year. They are living with cousins of mine, so I do not need to worry that they are not being looked after.'

'They will be married before you know it.' Keira remembered that Alima was always talking about how much she looked forward to her sons marrying and having children; Alima loved babies and small children.

Alima's face broke into delighted smiles. 'My eldest, Youssef, will be married this year, a girl from a family we know very well. Her mother and I have long wished for it, but Youssef insisted on choosing for himself. His father's death while he was just a boy has meant that Youssef has always thought of himself as a man; he insists on doing things his way. I was afraid he would not choose Lela, who is like my daughter already, but to my great joy he finally decided she was the wife he wanted.'

Keira laughed. 'I wonder if he was teasing you! So you may be a grandmother in a year or two!'

'If Allah wills it,' Alima said, her eyes shining. 'It is the dearest wish of my heart, and God is good, God is merciful.'

A few minutes later she followed her brother, after having helped Keira to unpack and put her clothes away. Keira closed the shutters again to exclude the heat of the day and keep the room cool for the night ahead, and sat down on the small, deeply upholstered sofa under the window to rest for a moment. The room's décor was Arab-inspired, a dressing-table with a charming Moorish arched mirror, elaborately carved chests in local woods, a brass bed covered with a geometric-patterned quilt made of soft cotton, the sheets bleached cotton, cool to the touch and beautifully laundered, piled high with feather pillows.

Everything was spotless; Alima was a very good housekeeper. Keira had always liked her, from the first time she had visited the villa. Disliking her stepfather, and ignored by her mother, Keira had spent a lot of her time in the kitchen talking to the servants.

That was how she came to learn some Arabic and even a little Berber, the vernacular spoken mainly now in the mountain regions of Morocco. Hassan's wife, the cook, was a Berber, and could switch from Arabic to her own childhood tongue in mid-flow but spoke almost no English. In the towns people had a mixture of European languages—French, Spanish and English were all spoken in hotels and restaurants although Arabic remained the tongue of the people.

'My name is Arabic for someone who loves music and dancing,' Alima had once told Keira proudly. 'And it is true of me; I love to sing and I play the flute; my father taught me—he was passionately fond of music. My boys play too, but neither of them can sing.'

In the evenings she sometimes played and sang for the family. She had a lovely voice, with that characteristic glottal stop which Arabs used for emphasis, a huskiness in low notes followed by a sudden trilling swoop upwards on higher notes. Since she would not take off the veil, even in front of her employer, she sang behind a fretted Arab screen at one end of the room, and she would never sing for strangers or visitors. Alima was a traditionalist, keeping to the old ways of her people, rarely leaving the house, and never unveiling in front of a man. When she had first begun working for Ivo Krensky he had attempted to persuade her, bribe her, into singing at some of the parties he gave in the villa for important and influential guests, but Alima had politely refused and, since her brother was invaluable to him, and Alima herself was so good at her job, Ivo had finally given up.

Ivo had lived in Morocco for years, but he still didn't grasp all the intricacies of the Arab way of life. He was a materialistic man, selfish, thoughtless, measuring everything by one yardstick—monetary value. He was not himself religious and did not understand people who were, and, since he believed that every man—and woman—had a price, he was always offending people for whom the law of Allah was paramount.

When Keira had rested for a while, she took a shower in the bathroom which led off her bedroom; it was Arab style too, white with dark blue patterning on the tiles, swirls running in a frieze along the top which, she remembered Alima telling her, were stylised symbols for trees and water, the most precious gifts of God, to a desert-living people.

Keira dressed in a loose caftan, made locally and bought on her last visit but left here, in the wardrobe in the bedroom. A pale cream weave, the material had gold threads glimmering in it.

She ate that evening in the dining-room, a magnificent room with echoing marble walls and floors, white damask tablecloths, silver candelabra and swinging silver lamps hung from chains in the ceiling. The air was full of exotic scents: the food cooking in the kitchen, the smell of flowers, incense burning to keep away insects.

Hassan's wife was expected to cook European dishes whenever Ivo Krensky was in residence; he was not inclined to culinary adventures and preferred plain food cooked without rich spices or sauces. Whenever Keira was there, she asked if she could try a speciality of the Maghreb—which was the name given to the great land mass composed of Morocco, Tunisia and Algeria. She had learnt that much of the food in the region was similar, a style of cooking born out of the ancient nomadic habits of the desert-wandering people who inhabited the area.

Hassan's wife, Yasmin, had remembered her pleasure in trying new foods, and had cooked a special meal for her first evening, starting with a light chicken soup made with rice, served in a silver tureen. Alima transferred a ladleful to her soup bowl and was going to give her another helping, but Keira stopped her hurriedly. She was still controlling her intake and eating slowly, as she had been taught at the clinic. Small helpings eaten at regular times were what she was aiming for.

'You don't like it?' Alima looked upset. The Moroccan women were unaware that she had an eating problem and she did not want to have to explain.

'It smells delicious but I have a very small appetite.'

Alima sighed. '*Chaha likom! Chaha tayiba!*' she said, a phrase Keira recognised as meaning something like the French phrase *bon appetit*, or the American version—enjoy!

Keira was careful to eat all the soup and Alima looked reassured. She brought in the main course, something called *hoot bcharmeela*, which turned out to be merely fish steaks smothered in a tomato sauce which, when Keira tasted it, was strongly flavoured with ginger and a trace of chilli. The fish was served with grilled sweet peppers, onions and tomatoes and rice cooked with the saffron which was so popular in Morocco.

Keira only had one small piece of fish, with a little pile of vegetables and rice; it was more than enough. She politely refused doughnuts made with orange juice and crushed hazelnuts, served in a sauce of honey and orange syrup. It looked intensely sticky and over-sweet, loaded with calories. Keira longed to taste them, but knew that if she ate one she would want more.

When she said so, Alima eagerly exclaimed, 'Have more! Have them all! You want to get a good husband, don't you? Men like women with curves like a snake, and you are made like a boy!'

'Perhaps tomorrow; I'm tired tonight, after my journey.' Keira suppressed the desire to tell her that she was not looking for a husband, not just yet, anyway.

Alima looked disappointed, but brought the usual mint tea which finished meals, instead of coffee. It was poured from high up, a cascading fountain of clear liquid from a curved spout, into a glass in a fretted silver holder. She sprinkled rose petals and honey into the tea before handing it formally to Keira, and then, while Keira slowly and ceremoniously sipped it, Alima sat down and played her flute and sang an old Moroccan folk song which she said shepherds sometimes sang to their flocks in the foothills of the Atlas mountains.

Keira felt quite sleepy afterwards; the music had been soothing and her nerves were calmer now than they had been for days. Before getting into bed she stood on the balcony of her room for a while, making sure she kept the glass door into her bedroom closely shut, to keep out insects. It was a warm moonlit night, the sky the colour of a purple grape with a tender bloom on it, the moon hanging on the velvety fabric of the night like a beaten silver disc with the marks of the hammer showing on the fine, thin surface.

The same moon would be shining down over London; but somehow it looked very different here where it did not compete with the reflection of the great city's millions of electric and neon lights.

Would Gerard Findlay even notice it, in his mews cottage? Or was he out tonight? He had broken with his last girlfriend months ago—had he got a new one yet?

Why did he kiss me? she wondered, her mind cloudy. The air was heavy with disturbing scents— the heavy perfume of roses, orange and lemon trees, olive and cypress—and insects buzzed around her, mosquitoes drawn by the heat of her soft skin, dive-bombing out of the moonlight. She swept them away, but knew she must go back indoors otherwise tomorrow she would be covered in bites.

From somewhere in the night she heard the high shrill of Arab singing and music, a rhythmic clapping keeping time with it, and a bazaar dog howling in the far distance.

London seemed a million miles away. Keira went to bed.

The following day Hassan and Yasmin drove her into Tangier and escorted her into the busy kasbah, through the winding maze of tiny alleys, some open to the noonday sun, others topped with fretted wooden roofs which gave some shade on the hottest days. Yasmin had her marketing to do—she wanted to visit an incredible spice shop which had row upon row of large glass jars full of ground or whole spices, some of them totally unknown to Keira. Keira wanted to buy a new caftan, some bangles and earrings, made by craftsmen who sat cross-legged in their shadowy, earth-floored shops, busily hammering away at gold or silver, and perhaps a pair of the delicate embossed leather sandals which were also made by local craftsmen.

Children ran around them everywhere they went, little brown hands held up for money, begging softly, smiling, their big dark eyes pleading. Hassan drove them away with sharp comments in Arabic and a firm flick of his fly-whisk, which was essential in the midday heat of the old city where, feeding on the openly displayed fruit and vegetables, flies buzzed relentlessly around and mosquitoes bred in the open drains and gutters.

Keira was sitting on a leather stool in a narrow, rather dark little shop, trying on sandals with the help of the shoe-maker's veiled wife, when she noticed a tall man in a white djellabah walking past. He had the hood of his garment raised over his head, but she caught sight of sleek black hair and a tanned, razor-edged profile, and her whole body jerked in shock.

Gerard Findlay?

He had gone before she could be sure her eyes weren't playing tricks on her. She got to her feet and went out of the shop to get a second look at him, but was too late. The man had vanished into one of the side-streets.

How could it be him? Keira told herself impatiently. What on earth would he be doing in Morocco? He's miles away, in London. You must have got it badly if you're starting to see him everywhere you go! Pull yourself together.

She paid for her sandals and she and Yasmin waited together while Hassan went to get the car, which he had parked, of course, outside the walled kasbah area. Keira couldn't help looking at every tall man in a djellabah who walked past; mostly they politely turned their heads away, to avoid looking at her just as the male shopkeepers in the souk spoke to Hassan, not to her, even when she herself asked a question.

She had put up her caftan hood, which served the double purpose of keeping the midday sun off and to some extent hiding her face. She might be wearing Arab dress but her fair skin, her vivid red hair and green eyes gave away her European origins. Of course, Moroccans were used to seeing European women walking about without the veil. Tourism was fast becoming one of their main sources of income although agriculture was still very important. Nevertheless Keira felt uncomfortable when she was stared at by passing men; she was very glad that she had Hassan and Yasmin with her.

She talked to Sara on the phone that evening before dinner. 'Are you sure you don't mind if Rashid comes?' Sara asked her.

'Of course I don't; there's plenty of room in the villa and I like Rashid; it will be more fun if we have a man here to escort us to places where two women couldn't go alone! You know what Arab countries are like.'

Sara giggled. 'Well, I should!'

Keira laughed too, but half apologised. 'I keep forgetting you're Arab yourself.'

'Well, I have lived in England most of my life!'

'Mind you, I always feel nervous if I'm out alone at night in London,' Keira said grimly. 'The streets simply aren't safe any more after dark.'

Later she asked, 'Do you know yet when you can come?'

'I still haven't had these tests at the hospital...'

'What are the tests for?' Keira asked anxiously.

'They think I may be slightly anaemic and having a baby makes that worse, apparently—babies take iron from the mother's blood; that's why they insist on a pregnant woman taking iron tablets. And they're worried about my bones——'

'Your bones?' interrupted Keira, even more worried. It sounded as if there was something seriously wrong with Sara.

'The doctor looked at my nails and teeth and thinks I have a calcium deficiency, and that's another problem—the baby draws on your calcium, too. I'd no idea about all this, did you?'

'Having a baby is a lot more complicated than I'd thought.'

Sara sighed. 'You're telling me! So I'm going to have to take a calcium supplement too—I shall rattle like a pill-box before I have this baby. They want to do tests to find out why I have these deficiencies and if there's an underlying problem with my health.' Sara sounded anxious herself. 'Rashid was very upset about all this, of course. He's such a worrier.'

'With good cause,' said Keira soberly. 'I'm worried about you too. Look, never mind about the holiday—we can always go on holiday some other time. The most important thing is for you to make sure you're OK.'

'The doctor thinks I haven't been eating properly for years,' Sara said wryly. 'Well, we don't, do we? Models are always dieting and some of the diets are crazy—the grapefruit diet, for instance. I was on that for weeks, eating nothing but grapefruit. I lost a lot of weight, but the doctor said I must have lost a lot of minerals and stuff as well, and now I'm paying for it.'

Keira had been given a very similar warning, not long ago, about the dangers of malnutrition.

'Well, make sure you take the doctor's advice—let me know how you get on, won't you?'

'I still hope to join you in Tangier; I'll keep in touch,' promised Sara before ringing off.

Keira went to bed early again that evening. She still hadn't acclimatised to the heat and humidity and found herself very tired by the end of the day. As usual, Alima had plugged an electric insect-killer into one of the electric points and the room was clear of mosquitoes.

The shutters were closed, the room cool, but Keira found herself unable to sleep. She kept remembering the moment in the shoe shop when she'd caught sight of the tall man in a djellabah striding past.

If it hadn't been Gerard it had looked exactly like him.

Oh, don't be so stupid! she told herself. Dark hair, tanned olive skin, a tall, thin figure—that description would fit millions of Moroccan men!

The memory of that kiss came back too, and her body began to burn with sensuality and an agonising desire. She tossed and turned, getting hotter every second. Never again, she thought; she couldn't bear to fall in love with him, knowing how it would end, the misery and pain of parting. She must stop thinking about him. When she got back to London she would avoid him.

After an hour the room seemed airless. The shutters were electronically operated; she pressed a button and they lifted, allowing moonlight to flood into the room. No need to switch on a light to see her way; she slid out of bed and padded barefoot to the double glass doors leading out onto the balcony. Sliding them open a fraction, she slipped between them, hurriedly shutting them again to keep out insects.

The view was magical by moonlight, the gardens shimmering in the silvery light, cypress trees making black exclamation marks across the deep blue sky, and in the distance Tangier, a city of minarets and domes with the glitter of stars around them, looking like an illustration from an oriental fairy-story.

Keira leaned on the rail of the balcony, staring out dreamily, feeling the soft air on her hot skin, blowing her fine lawn nightdress against her legs. Slowly she began to cool down, but just as she was about to go back inside and try again to sleep she saw something out of the corner of her eye, a movement among the palm trees bordering the drive. An animal?

She turned her head to stare, guessing that it must be one of the dogs that Hassan kept to deter intruders. At night they were allowed to roam the grounds. With Hassan or anyone they knew they could be lambs, but when confronted by a stranger they turned into dangerous, wolf-like creatures which could tear an intruder to pieces.

Hassan had warned her never to go out into the grounds once the dogs were let loose.

The dark shadow moved again while she stared, and her heart leapt into her mouth as she realised it was a man, not an animal, a man in a black Balaclava helmet and black clothes.

A burglar! Keira realised, turning to rush back indoors to raise the alarm, wake Alima and get her to warn Hassan.

'Keira!'

The deep, cool voice froze her in her tracks. She turned to look down and saw the man move out into the moonlight, pulling off the black Balaclava as he did so.

Her body quivered in fierce, primitive shock as she recognised him. It was Gerard Findlay.

He stepped out on to the lawn and stared up at her. She knew he could see her as clearly as she saw him; his mouth was curved in an odd, wry smile and his eyes were fixed on her. He was wearing a black tracksuit and running shoes and black gloves on his hands, and there was something looped over his shoulder—it looked like thin rope. She almost pinched herself to make sure she wasn't dreaming.

Suddenly from round the corner of the house a dog ran, snarling. Gerard took a swift look and broke into a lope towards her. Just below her balcony he paused, pulled something from his pocket, fumbling with paper wrapping. Keira dazedly watched as he flung a lump of meat towards the dog which had almost reached him. The great black and tan hound stopped dead, sniffing at the meat, then began to tear it wolfishly, swallowing chunks of it whole.

Keira felt totally unreal by now. She just stood there and watched, hypnotised by the whole bizarre, surreal nature of what was happening.

Gerard pulled the looped rope from his shoulder and whirled it round his head as if about to lasso something. It was only at that instant that Keira realised there was something metallic on the end of the rope. It flew towards her in a shining arc, and she jumped back in alarm, then heard it clink as it hit the rail of the balcony.

She could see it now, a three-pointed object made of steel; one point had caught behind the rail; Gerard pulled the rope taut and began to climb. Terrified, Keira leant over the balcony to watch him.

'You'll fall! That rope won't take your weight!'

She had barely got the words out when his head appeared level with the balcony and he climbed over the rail. Keira backed, her lips parted in a breathless gasp.

Below the dog had gulped down all the meat and began barking angrily up at them. Gerard deftly pulled up his rope, freed it from the rail, opened the glass door of Keira's room and threw the rope through to land on the floor with a faint clink.

'What on earth are you doing——?' she began, but his hand closed over her mouth, silencing her. He held her with one arm, hard against his body, lifted her feet off the floor and carried her, struggling, through the open windows, closed them then reached out with his free hand to press the button controlling the electric shutters which silently rolled shut again.

From outside they could both still hear the dog barking, then another dog joining in, and after another moment the sound of running feet, and Hassan's voice, talking in Arabic.

'Will you let me go? What is going on? What are you doing here?' said Keira under the muffling hand, and angrily tried to bite.

Gerard carried her further away from the window and deposited her on the bed, sitting down beside her, his hand still over her mouth.

Alima's voice joined in from her room down the corridor; she must have been looking out of the window, awakened by the barking of the dogs. She and her brother talked to each other in Arabic.

Keira wished she knew what they were saying, but the few polite phrases she had picked up were not adequate for an occasion like this.

She glared up at Gerard over his muffling hand; he was staring down at her, his grey eyes brilliant, flecked with the moonlight filtering through the closed shutters. The fixity of his focus on her made a sliver of ice trickle down her spine, and her stomach clenched in sudden, intense sensual awareness. Terror split the sky of her mind—if he touched her she would not be able to control her reactions; she would betray herself, he would realise what he could do to her and he would despise her.

Gerard slowly lifted his hand from her mouth, still holding her with the lance of his stare; his fingers slid down to grip her chin and tilt it upwards, and he bent towards her. She wanted to move away, to escape, to cry out, bring Hassan and his sister running to her aid, but she couldn't; she was transfixed, hypnotised by those silvery, compelling eyes.

His mouth touched hers and fire ran through her veins; she tasted the heady sweetness of desire on her tongue and her head swam; she felt as if she was weightless, floating. Her eyes shut; she abandoned herself as the passion flared between them like fire through brushwood.

She never knew afterwards whether Gerard pushed her backwards or she fell, but somehow she was lying on the bed a moment later, with his lean, hard body on top of her; her nightdress had ridden up and Gerard's hand was caressing the soft skin of her thigh and hip.

She groaned, heard the zip of his tracksuit top being pulled down; he shed it, the rest of his clothes, and was naked above her. Her heart began to pulse in mingled hunger and shock, and at that instant she heard a sound outside in the corridor, the shuffle of slippered feet on the woodblock floor.

Gerard tensed, lifting his head.

'Who's that?' he whispered.

'Alima—the housekeeper,' Keira said, trembling violently and unable to look at him. She was so fiercely aware of his nakedness, the smooth tanned flesh touching her; her mouth was dry with passion and angry shame because she knew she wanted him and she hoped desperately that he had not guessed how much.

'Damn,' he muttered, scowling. His eyes shot compulsion at her. 'Sound sleepy...make her think you've slept through all the noise, tell her you haven't seen or heard a thing. You can't let her in.' He moved slightly, his long thigh moving against hers. 'Can you?'

Flame enveloped her face, her throat. Of course she couldn't; it would destroy her reputation if Alima or any of the servants saw a naked man in her room. Of course, she could scream now, and tell them that he had broken in here to attack her— but Hassan would insist on calling the police and how could she pretend he was a stranger when he lived next door to her in London, a fact that the police would rapidly establish?

Alima tapped on the door and both Gerard and Keira lay very still for a second.

Feeling his grey eyes watching her, glittering in the dark, their warning unmistakable, Keira knew she had no choice but to do as he had ordered.

Huskily she called out, 'What is it?' The shake in her voice could be put down to having just woken up. 'What's wrong?'

'Oh, miss... The dogs have been barking but Hassan cannot see any signs of entry on the ground floor. You haven't heard anything, have you, miss?'

'I've only just woken up,' she lied. 'My shutters are closed; I can't hear a thing through them.'

'Perhaps the dogs were chasing an owl; there is a family of them living in an old stable in the grounds. They frighten the dogs and make them bark. I told Hassan that must be it, but he insisted that I check that you were OK. I am sorry to have disturbed you, miss; can I get you anything? A drink?'

'No, thank you, I'm too sleepy. Goodnight, Alima.'

'Goodnight, miss.'

Alima's sandals flapped along towards the head of the stairs, she was no doubt going down to talk to her brother. As soon as the house fell silent again Gerard sat up and put on his clothes while Keira watched, her body cooling now, the passion all gone, her head a whirl of suspicion, doubt and alarm. She looked up at him through the shadows of the room, her green eyes cat-like, narrowed, hostile.

His lovemaking had had a cool purpose, she angrily realised; he had been making sure she would not call out, have him arrested. He had made a fool of her, and she felt hatred surge through her veins.

'What are you really doing, breaking into the villa?' she broke out in scathing accusation. 'Are you a thief, after some of my stepfather's collection? It can't be a coincidence...you turning up at this villa, when you live in one of Ivo's London properties. You broke into my cottage in London too—and when you'd gone I noticed a photograph missing; I know it had been there that morning, so I know you must have taken it. It was a photo of this villa, wasn't it? And my stepfather's collection! What's going on? What are you up to?'

CHAPTER FOUR

'YOU'RE very observant,' he drawled, running a hand through his thick black hair. 'Yes, I took one of your photos—I wanted one of you but I couldn't make up my mind which was the best. Then I heard your key in the front door so I had to snatch one and go. I just grabbed the nearest one, which turned out to be a picture of you with your mother and stepfather . . . what's his name again?'

'Ivo Krensky,' she said, not believing a word he had just told her, her green eyes flashing contempt and defiance at him. 'And you're a liar. I don't know what you're up to, but I'd put money on it that you're up to something. Just get out of here, will you?'

His brows arched. 'While those killer dogs are prowling around down there?'

Her voice shook with the force of her anger against him. 'I hope they get you. I hope they tear you to pieces, chew you up and spit you out!'

His mouth curled in mocking amusement. 'Charming. And if I do try to leave while they're prowling around down there I've no doubt that that would be what happened—which is why I'm staying put for the moment.'

'Not in here!' Keira scrambled off the bed and reached for a lawn wrap which matched her nightdress, hurriedly put it on and tied the belt around her slender waist while Gerard watched her coolly as if she were putting on a show for his enjoyment.

Her mind was working faster now that they were both dressed and the tense intimacy of those moments on the bed had ended. Without haste, she moved over to the window and pressed the button to open the shutters again; moonlight flooded the room, dazzling her. She turned to look at him, her chin lifted.

'If you don't leave I'm going to start screaming.' She pulled open the glass windows as she finished speaking and the sound of barking came up to them both. The dogs were still out there, although they sounded as if they had moved further away.

'Your stepfather is in Florida, isn't he?'

She stared, frowning, alert to every nuance in his voice. 'How do you know that? What's your interest in Ivo?' How had he found out where she was staying? Who would have had the address of this villa? 'Did Sara tell you where I was?'

'Sara? No. I would have asked her but I didn't know where to find her.'

Of course, he was a reporter, used to doing research on people; he had access to all sorts of supposedly private information. These days everything was on computer somewhere—how much someone earned, how long they had been married, where they were born, even which dentist they visited. If you knew how to access computerised information you could find out anything.

'I know he and your mother are in Florida—and you're here all alone.' The deep, husky voice sent shivers down her spine, made her mouth go dry.

'The villa is full of servants!' She was suddenly very relieved about that. What if she had been alone when he'd broken in here? Her breathing quickened as she remembered his body pressing her down on the bed, the brush of his naked flesh, his mouth moving against her own. If Alima hadn't come along... She shuddered at what might have happened next.

'I imagine they're essential—this villa is huge. But then your stepfather is very rich, isn't he? How did he make his money, by the way?' Gerard sat down on the bed again, his lean body no less formidable for being totally at ease, the wide shoulders and deep chest, the slim hips and long, long legs promising power and sensuality. Few women would be able to ignore that promise; Keira certainly couldn't, although she fought against the magnetic drag of the attraction, tried not to look at him too often.

'I'm not discussing my stepfather with you,' she said curtly. 'Now, will you leave, or do I start screaming?'

His grey eyes gleamed at her in the moonlight, his skin smooth and golden, and her pulses went haywire, her breathing fast, ragged because it was not his sexual allure that seriously disturbed her. No, it was the emotional threat of falling in love with him that she dreaded, and when he smiled at her like that she knew it could happen, she could completely lose her head over him, and that was the path to pain and humiliation, to making a fool of herself, to being laughed at or pitied. She could not bear the thought of either.

'Will you get out of here?' she asked angrily.

He locked his hands behind his head, lounging on the bed casually, watching her.

'You do know,' he drawled, 'that the moon is right behind you and the moonlight is streaming through your nightdress and robe, making them totally transparent? Standing there like that, you might as well be naked.'

Aghast, she shot away from the window, and heard him laughing softly.

'Why did you move?' he reproached. 'You have a ravishing body—a little too thin for my taste, but I gather the camera adds pounds, and photographers insist on having skinny models. Pity about that. Have you ever done nude photography? I know some models do; even Marilyn Monroe posed for a calendar nude, I believe.'

'Well, I haven't and I wouldn't,' Keira snapped, her face burning. She was disturbed by what was on his mind—all this talk of nakedness and bodies.

'I'm glad to hear it,' he approved, and, contrarily, she bristled with resentment.

'Don't patronise me!' Her green eyes mere slits of fierce suspicion, she bit out, 'Are you doing a story on me? Why all these personal questions about me and my family? What are you hoping to find out? And how about explaining what you're doing here, at this villa, in the middle of the night, in Tangier, when I last saw you in London?'

'I followed you here,' he said softly.

Keira's heart missed a beat, a heavy thud that made her feel dizzy. If he had followed her here it would not have been personal—how could it be? They hardly knew each other. But, all the same, yearning made her tremble. All her life there had been a black hole inside her, an emptiness she was still waiting to fill. Even as a very small child she had known that nobody loved her, nobody really cared whether she lived or died; it had been an intensely lonely existence.

Oh, she had had clothes, food, a comfortable home—but for any human being mere material comfort was never enough. Let alone a child. The need for love had been agonising at times; when it was too much to bear she had started to eat for comfort. At first it had just been sweets, then when she'd reached puberty she'd begun to eat anything she could find. That was when the real problem had begun—when she was about twelve, she remembered. Food had become a drug to her, numbing the pain of being unloved, unwanted, the bleak loneliness she had increasingly felt. She had begun to spend all her pocket money on food. Her mother was generous, at least, with money; she'd given Keira ludicrously large amounts and never asked her what she spent it on. Keira had hidden food in her bedroom, and when she had eaten that she would creep down to the kitchen and steal food to take back upstairs where she would cram it into her mouth, eating as if possessed, crouching in her bed, with the door locked, until the fit passed.

Then the guilt and fear would start; she would be terrified of getting fat because she knew she would have no chance of love at all if she wasn't as beautiful as her mother. Everyone kept telling her so, and she could see it was true.

To be loved you had to be beautiful. Her father had loved her mother, and so did Ivo. Everywhere they went, Keira had seen men turn their heads and stare when her mother walked by. She'd believed that if she was ever to have a hope of being loved she must stay slim, so after eating she'd begun to go into the bathroom and make herself sick. She couldn't actually remember when it had all started but the pattern had been established long before anyone else noticed it.

'What are you thinking?' Gerard asked, and she started, dragging herself back from a bitter past to find him watching her as intently as a hawk on the wing watching a movement on the ground below. His body was poised and alert, his eyes hooded and gleaming.

She shivered. 'How did you find out where I was?'

Coolly, he told her, 'I asked the agent.'

It was that simple! No tremendous research, no mysterious powers—he just asked the house agent!

'I looked out of the window and saw you leaving in a taxi with your luggage,' he went on. 'I rang the agent to ask if they knew where you had gone, and they said you were staying in your stepfather's place in Tangier, so I decided to come here for a holiday myself. By coincidence, my office have ordered me to take a break; they don't want me back at work yet.' His voice changed and his face darkened. He frowned blackly. 'The stupid bastards won't send me abroad with a camera team again until I'm fully recovered.'

Distracted by what he had said, her green eyes ran over him, searching for visible signs of his injuries. She had noticed several scars on his body, but they seemed quite healed—thin, livid weals against his healthy brown skin.

'I remember hearing that you had been shot,' she said slowly. 'I never heard the details. What happened exactly?'

He shrugged indifferently. 'A bullet parted my hair.' He bent his head forward and swept his hair back, showing her the thin seam of raised skin where the bullet had ploughed.

Keira came forward slowly, staring at it; she wanted to touch it gently with her fingertip, stroke it—but she fought the temptation.

'It looks painful,' she said huskily.

He shrugged. 'Not any more. Just a flesh wound; it's well-healed. I was also shot in the leg and now I limp sometimes, especially in wet weather; I'm not sure why rain affects it but it does. Another bullet just missed a lung—do you want to see the scar?' His eyes mocked her, glinting with laughter.

'No,' she said hurriedly as he showed signs of unzipping his tracksuit-top, and he grinned.

Suddenly angry, Keira burst out, 'Why on earth do you do things like that? I mean, going to trouble spots, war zones, knowing you might get into the line of fire. I'd be scared of being killed.'

'I'm terrified of being killed,' he assured her drily. 'I'm a devout coward, believe me.'

'I don't believe you!' she snapped. 'If you were you wouldn't be a war correspondent, and I've seen you on TV in really hairy situations, as cool as a cucumber, talking as if you were standing in Piccadilly Circus!'

'Some war zones are safer than Piccadilly in the rush-hour,' he joked, but she wasn't amused. It was too disturbing to be funny.

He considered her wryly. 'Look, if you're to survive long as a war correspondent you need a very strong sense of danger. It's the brave ones who get themselves blown up. Cowards like me know that any risk has to be calculated to within an inch, and *then* count to ten before you go in!'

'Is that why you broke in here tonight?' she asked, quick as a flash. 'I bet you knew there were guard dogs patrolling the grounds at night—and how did you get past the electronic barrier? Why didn't you set off any of the alarms?'

He grinned at her, visibly pleased with himself. 'I climbed over the wall before the security system was switched on. It doesn't come into operation until it's dark. I got in just before that, at dusk. I climbed a tree and spent several uncomfortable hours up there, waiting for all the lights in the house to go out.'

'Why?' she asked, stunned by this revelation. 'What on earth is this all about? What is it you want?'

She was only a few feet away from him by then; he shot out a hand, his fingers closed round her wrist and he pulled her towards him. She gave a helpless cry of shock and dismay but couldn't stop herself falling forward, into the waiting arms.

'No, don't . . .' she cried out, trying to push him away yet at the same time instantly aware of the male power of the body she lay against, the muscled legs, the rhythmic rise and fall of his chest, the very masculine scent of his skin, musky and sensual, arousing barbaric reactions deep inside her own body.

'You asked me what I wanted,' he whispered, his fingertips stroking her cheek, delicately following the parted, quivering line of her mouth, sliding down her throat. 'It was this...' His mouth lightly brushed her eyes and she shut them, taking a long, painful breath. Inch by tantalising inch his mouth crawled down her cheek and desire began to twist inside her, so intense that it was like a knife wound, burning, tormenting. His lips reached hers, touched briefly, lifted, came down again, lifted again, the contact fleeting, light, teasing, like having a moth flutter against you and fly away again.

Almost maddened, she muttered, 'Stop it!' and tried to break free, but then he took her face between his hands and looked down at her, the moonlight making his eyes mirrors which reflected her in their silvery depths but did not show her what lay behind his stare.

'I want you,' he murmured. 'That's why I'm here, Keira. I want you, and you want me too, don't you? There's no mistaking it when it's mutual; the air sizzles.'

The soft words made her stiffen as if he had hit her. She came so abruptly out of the sensual daze in which she had been suspended for the last few minutes that she was as giddy as if she were a deep-sea diver brought up too fast from the depths of the sea.

He knew. He knew he only had to touch her with one fingertip for her to tremble and feel faint. Anguish washed through her.

'No!' She took him by surprise, stumbling off the bed in a lurch of fear.

Gerard got up too, uncoiling like a snake about to strike, his lean, black-clad body lethal in the moonlight.

'You know it's true, Keira. We both know.'

'Go away, get out!' She wanted to scream, but she dared not; she had to keep her voice low or Alima and Hassan would hear them. It would be embarrassing if they knew she had a man in her bedroom. They would be shocked. However angry she might be with Gerard, it was out of the question for her to call the police, and once Hassan and his sister knew that they would assume that Gerard was her lover. It would radically change the way they treated her, she could be certain of that. Their code of morals was different from her own, she did not share their religious beliefs, but she valued their good opinion. And it wasn't true either—Gerard wasn't her lover, and she had no intention that he ever would be.

She backed and he followed quietly, step by dangerous step, watching her intently.

'I'm not sleeping with you,' she said desperately.

'You aren't a virgin, are you?'

She blushed a hot pink and looked at him with rage. 'That's no business of yours! And it has nothing to do with it. I don't want to sleep with you, that's why I'm refusing! You may be conceited enough to think that every woman who meets you can't wait to jump into bed with you—but not me. I don't want to sleep with you, got that?'

His mouth twisted. 'I hear what you're saying, but it contradicts what I know you're feeling.'

'Really! You are the most . . .' Adjectives seethed in her head: maddening, infuriating, selfish, arrogant . . .

She had backed herself up against a wall; he stood in front of her, barring the way of escape.

'The most what?' he said, lifting a hand to lay a long index finger against the side of her neck. It was the lightest possible touch, but she tensed as if an electric shock had flashed through her, her body alight immediately, and could have screamed, knowing that he felt her reaction and was picking up the wild beating of her pulse.

She pushed his hand away. 'Leave me alone!'

'Why is your heart beating so fast?' he murmured.

She swallowed and he watched the convulsive movement of her long, pale throat.

'Why are you breathing as if you've been running a marathon?'

Her lips were bone-dry; she moistened them with the tip of her tongue and he watched that, his grey eyes brilliant with excitement.

'I want to do that,' he whispered. 'I love the taste of your mouth.' And he bent before she could stop him and ran the tip of his tongue along her lips, sending waves of sensuality flooding through her.

She pulled her head back, her eyes wild and terrified. 'Stop it, please stop this. I want you to go. I hardly know you—we may have seen each other quite often, going in and out of our homes, but we haven't actually met more than three or four times.'

He nodded, his mouth curling wryly. 'That's true. What difference does it make, though? The very first time I saw you, you made quite an impression on me. I noticed the way you moved; I thought you must be a dancer, you were so graceful.'

She stood still, listening but afraid to believe what she heard. How much of this did he mean?

'But I had just had a bad experience with a woman,' he shrugged. 'She was an unfaithful little bitch and left me feeling pretty raw about your sex. I was in a bad mood for most of the time when I first moved into the mews. Then I flew out on that assignment and I didn't see you again for months. So I didn't realise how much I fancied you until I broke into your house the other day, not knowing if I'd find a corpse inside.'

She shuddered at the memory, turning her head aside in a bleak gesture of denial.

'Don't talk about that.'

There was a silence then he gently said, 'I agree; let's talk about the future, not the past. But I do want to hear more about you; that's why I came— to get to know you better. Will you have lunch with me tomorrow in Tangier? At my hotel? I've hired a car; I'll drive out here to pick you up at about eleven?'

She would have said anything to get him to go. She nodded, her lashes down over her green eyes.

His hand shot out and caught her chin, tilted her head so that she had to look up at him.

'I want your word on that,' he said drily, and she read in his face the knowledge that she had not meant to keep the appointment. She couldn't lie with those hard eyes watching her.

'Oh, very well—you have my word,' she muttered, thinking, Well, having lunch in a Tangier hotel is innocuous enough, isn't it? What harm can there be in that? But she already sensed the danger in keeping that appointment—she felt the feverish excitement pulsing through her now. The more she saw of him, the more he might come to mean to her, and she was afraid to take that risk. 'I'll be here,' she said, though, knowing he would not leave until he had her promise.

'If you aren't, I'll find you, no matter how long it takes.'

There was an odd silence after that; they both stared at each other as if the words had a resonance neither of them had expected, as if suddenly they both felt a shift in their relationship.

Keira felt herself trembling. His threat revealed something about him that her own nature responded to with a leap of empathy. The words were the man himself: obsessive, fierce, passionate.

Huskily, he said, 'I mean that, so don't forget it.' Turning away, he went out on to the balcony and hooked his rope to the balcony rail. There was no sound now of the dogs. They must be round the other side of the house again.

He pulled his Balaclava back over his face, put on his gloves, climbed on to the rail, then glanced back at Keira, his eyes gleaming slits in the dark material covering the rest of his face.

'Goodnight.' His dark body swung over the side a second later, and he dropped out of sight, absailing down the villa at great speed. Keira heard the soft thud as he touched the ground, then with a jerk he detached his spike and the rope vanished downwards.

Keira ran to stare down over the balcony. She made no sound and yet Gerard sensed her there;

he turned his head to shoot a glance up at her, raised his hand silently in parting, then began to lope away across the lawns towards the trees on the perimeter. His shadow slid between them a moment later and was engulfed by blackness.

Keira looked up at the starry sky, resenting the beauty of the night and the emptiness of space beyond the stars because it echoed the aching need she never quite forgot. When she grew up she had hoped, at last, to find the love she had never been given as a child, and the way she looked had certainly meant that she had always had plenty of male attention, but it had never been the right sort. Men always wanted her for the wrong reasons—they wanted her body, they fantasised about her, they used her looks to boost their own ego, impressing their friends and colleagues by having a girl who looked like her on their arm at parties or dining out. The one thing they did not offer was a love as deep as the need she felt. Most men, she had discovered, were embarrassed by intense emotions; they feared them. How would Gerard Findlay react if——?

She broke off, biting her lip. Stop it! she told herself. Don't even think about loving him. You don't even really know what he's up to, arriving here, out of the blue.

He was a reporter, she mustn't forget that. He could have any number of reasons for following her to Tangier. She was a well-known face, after the TV advertisements for Rexel; she was no stranger to the gossip columns and Gerard could be secretly planning to do a big story on her. The newspapers hadn't got on to her loss of the con-

tract yet. Rexel meant to announce that only after
a board meeting they were having that week, at
which they would decide precisely what they meant
to do about the next year's TV commercials. Maybe
Gerard planned to do a story about her being
dumped by Rexel, coupling that with news of her
bulimia, and he had followed her out here to see
what else he could dig up.

One thing she was certain about—all her instincts screamed it—Gerard had a hidden agenda.
She could not trust him, and she had to defend
herself against both him and her own emotions.

Bleakly, she turned away from the moonlit night,
the warmly breathing beauty of the gardens, went
back into her room, closed the shutters, climbed
into bed, and eventually went to sleep.

Alima woke her up at eight with a tray of
breakfast, which she ate out on the balcony, in her
wrap, watching the sunlit morning—birds flew
across the lawns, sang in the trees and the roses
began to breathe a warm perfume in the sunshine.
Hassan had already been out earlier, to turn on the
sprinkler system, spraying the roses and lawns,
which now glistened as if with dew.

Keira ate a simple breakfast—coffee, freshly
squeezed orange juice, half a roll thickly spread with
Alima's own home-made marmalade, the oranges
for which had grown here, in this garden. The con-
fection had a bittersweet taste and was full of grated
orange-rind.

'Delicious marmalade,' Keira told her and Alima
beamed.

'Have more. Eat whole roll; you don't
eat enough.'

'I'm not very hungry in the mornings—oh, and I shall be out to lunch today.'

'Out to lunch?' Alima looked surprised and curious; she knew Keira knew very few people in Tangier, only friends of her stepfather and mother, none of whom she liked very much. 'You want Hassan to drive you somewhere?'

'No, a friend from England will be calling for me, at eleven. His name is Findlay, Gerard Findlay.'

'A friend from England,' repeated Alima, frowning. 'A Mr Findlay? A family friend? Your mother knows him?' Her instincts were to worry about Keira going anywhere alone with a man, even though she knew Keira lived in a very different way in London. Alima had seen plenty of films of life in England and America, but here, in Tangier, Keira was expected to be far more careful, and, usually, she went along with that protective attitude.

So now she had to descend to being evasive and she didn't enjoy the experience. She did not want to lie to Alima, but she knew Alima would only worry if she knew the truth.

'He is a tenant of Mr Krensky's, in London; he lives in one of my stepfather's properties.'

'And he is visiting Tangier at the same time as you?' Alima's voice held soft, veiled questions; her eyes held hints and implications, too. To her if a man who was known to the family followed Keira out to Tangier he must be an accepted suitor, the husband-to-be Alima had been waiting for Keira to produce ever since she left her teens behind.

Keira knew she was blushing and hurriedly turned away. 'I'll take a shower now, Alima, and get dressed.'

Alima left the room with her breakfast tray, smiling to herself, now completely convinced that she would soon be meeting Keira's future husband. That blush could only have one meaning!

In the shower Keira stood with closed eyes under the cool water, delighting in the feel of it on her hot skin. Gerard Findlay's arrival had complicated what might otherwise have been a peaceful week. Alima and her brother were going to start imagining all sorts of things—they would believe she was probably going to marry Gerard. They were bound to tell her mother about his visit, and then Elise and Ivo would start asking questions.

Anger stirred inside her. Damn Gerard! She had questions of her own she would like answered. Why had he really stolen that photo of her mother and Ivo? If he wasn't trying to extract a story about her, was he after a story about Ivo?

Plenty of other journalists had tried to find out more about Ivo. Her stepfather was something of a mystery man. He had millions, owned properties all over the world—yet nobody seemed to know much about him, other than that he claimed he was of Russian descent and hinted that he had royal blood, was somehow related to the Romanovs. Keira had never believed that for an instant!

Ivo always talked about having been involved in financial dealings in the States—talked about New York and Wall Street and the American stock market, the Dow Jones index, and said he still owned a large portfolio of stocks and shares.

Perhaps it was all true, but he also claimed he had owned a big manufacturing company somewhere in Ohio, and at different times had said he had lived in California, Texas and Seattle. It was impossible to pin him down on any of his various stories; he simply turned sullen and glowered at you if you asked too many questions.

There was nobody else you could ask, either. Ivo had no relations, and, although he had many acquaintances, he had few close friends and almost no old friends of long standing, so far as Keira was aware.

None of this bothered her mother. Elise didn't care who Ivo was, or had been, or how he had made his money, so long as he spent it on her now. Like a cat that had finally found the silk cushion and bowls of cream it had hankered for all its life, Elise was too busy purring to ask her husband any questions about himself.

Keira stepped out of the shower and dried herself, frowning. She would have to hope that Sara and Rashid arrived soon; once they were staying in the villa too she would be able to deal with Gerard.

She stood in her white towelling robe checking through her wardrobe, trying to decide what to wear, settling at last on a lemon silk suit, a long-sleeved, hip-length tunic top with large gold buttons marching up to the high neckline, the trousers very comfortable to wear, their loose folds flowing to her ankle.

Alima approved, giving her a delighted nod when she came downstairs later.

'Oh, that is very elegant, very pretty.'

'It was designed by an Arab, a cousin of my friend who hopes to join me here—Sara Ounissi.' Sara had given it to Keira as a Christmas present last year; she had bought it on discount from her cousin.

'She is married, you said?'

Keira nodded. 'Her husband may come with her. He wasn't intending to, but Sara has just found out that she is pregnant, so Rashid is worried about letting her come alone.'

'It is their first child?' Alima smiled a little wistfully. 'My husband was the same with our first baby; he was afraid something would go wrong and hardly let me put my foot to the ground. My mother-in-law lived with us and made me stay in bed half the day. Between the two of them I hardly moved for the nine months I carried Youssef. Thank heavens, with the next one it was all different. My mother-in-law was too busy taking care of Youssef for me; he was her pet and her darling, and I think she resented the very idea of me having another baby to compete with him—and my husband no longer worried about me. He took our second baby for granted.'

'You must tell Sara all that; it will be very reassuring for her.'

Alima laughed. 'You will find out yourself one day—may it be soon, in the mercy of Allah.'

Keira crossly felt herself blushing again.

'Do you want more coffee?' asked Alima, smiling.

Keira shook her head and went into the marble-floored reception-room, sat down on one of the deep, comfortable sofas to read a paperback novel she had bought at Heathrow on the journey here. It was hard to concentrate on the labyrinthine convolutions of the detective story; she kept forgetting who the various suspects were and why they might have murdered the victim. Every few pages she would put the book down and stare out at the sunlit garden, watching the dark shadows of birds flit from tree to tree, from bush to bush.

Promptly at eleven Gerard Findlay drove through the gates in a small white sports car with the top down, and drew up outside the house. Keira went out to meet him. She had collected a lemon silk stole, a long, fringed scarf, from her room earlier, and was wearing it over her head and draped across one shoulder. If they were going to drive with the car roof down, she was afraid her hair would be blown to bits, for one thing—and, for another, the stole matched her lemon suit and had made Alima smile with pleasure. Alima was always worried when she saw Keira going out without her head covered, with her face unhidden. Keira had no intention of wearing the full veil, but she was ready to compromise if it made Alima feel happier.

Gerard had climbed out of his car. He met her on the path, his dark hair wind-blown, his shirt worn without a tie and open at the collar, revealing tanned skin and a powerful throat, looking casual and devastatingly male.

Intense awareness flashed between them like electricity sparking; every time she saw him again her body leapt with sensuality, fiercely responding to him.

He stared at her, his face almost blank for a second, then said huskily, 'You look very lovely this morning.'

'Thank you.' Keira fought not to blush, and lost.

Gerard looked past her into the villa; the front door stood open and Hassan and Alima watched them from it, their dark eyes assessing him.

'I hoped you would ask me in for a cup of coffee and show me round the house,' he said, and Keira gave him a quick, frowning glance, immediately suspicious of his motives and what lay behind the suggestion. Was this what he really wanted? To look round Ivo's home, find out more about him from his possessions?

Coolly, she shrugged. 'Of course—come in.'

He was going to be disappointed. Ivo's private suite was the only part of the house that held anything personal to him—his very valuable collection of paintings and antiques, his office, his filing cabinets which no doubt contained details of his business life, his letters and everything else which Ivo wished to remain secret, including the hidden safes in which he kept Elise's jewellery when they were in residence. Whatever Gerard was after he would find in there—but the suite was always kept locked. Gerard would find out nothing about Ivo from the furniture and décor of the rest of the house, other than that Ivo was a very rich man with a good interior decorator.

CHAPTER FIVE

HASSAN and his sister greeted Gerard with the usual grave courtesy that they showed visitors to the house. Her dark eyes gleaming above her veil, Alima stood back and silently watched Gerard as he talked to her brother.

'You have just arrived in Tangier, sir?' Hassan asked, and got a nod in reply. 'You live in one of Mr Krensky's houses in London?' That got another smiling nod, then, to Keira's incredulity, Gerard said something in Arabic. Of course, this delighted Hassan, who answered in his own tongue, his usually serious face lighting up.

Keira stood listening to them talking away, wondering what they were saying. How typical of Gerard Findlay to be able to speak Arabic! She herself only knew a few words and found it very hard to manage the throat sounds which made Arabic such a different language. Gerard managed them with infuriating ease. Of course, being a foreign correspondent, he must have found it helpful to be able to speak languages—he probably knew a little of most of the European ones. At least enough to get by with when he was sent to do a story abroad. But Arabic was far more difficult.

Keira had a smattering of several European languages. The European Common Market had made an astonishing change in the attitude of the English towards learning languages. They had always been too lazy to bother, relying on other nations to speak English, but now that they travelled more, worked in other countries, or wanted to sell their goods to other European nations, they needed to be able to talk to people in those countries. These days most English people learnt French or German at school, but many also spoke a little Spanish because holidays there were so popular, some spoke Italian or Dutch or one of the Scandinavian languages, and Russian was increasingly popular because it had opened up to the West since the breaking up of the Soviet Union.

Alima turned to her after a few moments, excitement in her eyes. 'My brother has offered to show Mr Findlay around the house—I will make coffee; will you come and choose which cups you want to use?'

Keira knew from her voice that Alima could not wait to get her alone to talk about Gerard.

'I ought to go with them,' she said uncertainly. She trusted Hassan implicitly, but she did not trust Gerard. If he could manage it, he'd try to coax Hassan into showing him the locked suite. She was absolutely convinced that he was here for some secret purpose—but what?

Gerard had heard her; he turned to give her a dry, mocking look. 'Yes, come with us.'

Keira caught Hassan's eye and knew that he would rather she did not go with them. He enjoyed being in charge of the house, showing a visitor around it.

She hesitated, then said, 'No, I think I'll help Alima.'

Hassan relaxed again and smiled approval at her.

I ought not to give in to him like this, she thought. I'm not an Arab girl, or in his charge; I'm an adult woman with a mind of my own, so why am I letting him make my decisions for me? Oh, well, I'm only here for a short holiday, and I like Hassan and his family; I don't want to upset or disturb them.

Gerard's grey eyes were coolly amused; he had read her dilemma, he knew she didn't trust him and wanted to keep an eye on him, yet had not felt she could insist on accompanying him and Hassan around the villa in the face of Hassan's obvious disapproval.

She threw him back a defiant, impatient look. He needn't smile at her like that. OK, she wanted Hassan and Alima to approve of her! That was none of his business. It was an instinct buried too deep for her to be able to get at it and work out what it sprang from. She didn't know why she was uneasy when someone she liked looked at her with disapproval. Maybe it was an intrinsic part of being female, or maybe it was social conditioning from birth, but however the habit had begun it was now entrenched, would take years of therapy to alter and Keira couldn't be bothered to take it that seriously.

Hassan said something in Arabic, waving a hand towards the stairs, and Gerard gave her a crooked little smile.

'I must tear myself away from you, then.'

Keira was furious to see Hassan and Alima pick up on that remark, looking at each other quickly with secret smiles.

She felt like poking her tongue out at Gerard, but decided instead to turn the tables on him by saying soulfully, 'Well, don't leave me alone for too long!'

His eyes gleamed with laughter as he turned to follow Hassan. Keira and Alima went in the opposite direction towards the kitchen. Alima began chattering excitedly to her sister-in-law in Arabic. Keira laid a tray while the other two women made coffee, arranged food on a silver cake-stand. Yasmin had baked *fkoss*, a sweet bread flavoured with caraway, poppy and aniseed, *el briouat*, which were pastries shaped like croissants and filled with almond paste, and some tiny biscuits full of dates and crushed nuts.

'He is very handsome—is he rich?' asked Alima.

'I don't imagine so.' Keira spoke in repressive tones, trying to convey disapproval of the question.

Alima breathed a regretful sigh. 'Does he have many brothers and sisters?'

'I have no idea.'

Alima looked shocked. 'You do not know his family?'

'Not yet.' Keira gave her a resigned glance. 'We do things differently in England, Alima. Our families are not so involved in our lives. We choose our own partners.'

The coffee had percolated; Alima had to deal with that before she went on talking, then she turned to relay what Keira had said to her sister-in-law, who looked horrified. The two women began talking at the same time, interrupting each other, not listening to what the other was saying.

Keira took the chance to escape. She found Gerard and Hassan wandering through the ground floor. As she appeared, Hassan excused himself and went towards the kitchen to oversee the preparation for coffee.

'Miss me?' mocked Gerard.

She gave him a cold look. 'I didn't know you spoke Arabic; you didn't tell me.'

'It never came up. I once spent a year in Cairo; I even learnt a little Coptic.'

'Well, aren't you clever?' she muttered and he laughed.

'Languages come easy to me.'

'What a surprise. I suppose most things do.'

'Not women,' he drawled.

She gave him a furious green-eyed look. 'Don't drag sex into this again. What were you doing in Cairo?'

He was grinning like a Cheshire cat. She wanted to slap him. 'Working as a newspaper correspondent and studying the architecture and history of Egypt.'

What a surprising man he was! She had the feeling that she had barely scraped the surface of his nature so far. There was a great deal hidden below that very macho façade, the man of action one saw on TV with snipers firing around him and shells landing in ruined houses while he talked to the camera very fast, as if he might have to run like hell any minute. That man had many other layers; she couldn't even guess what he might be hiding.

Gerard was walking about, staring at the marble floors, the chandeliers, the deep brocade sofas and oriental lacquered furniture. Crossing to a wall, he studied some paintings hanging there. Over his shoulder he said, 'Your stepfather likes modern art,

I see. I admire his taste—he's got a wonderful little Klee here.'

Keira walked over to join him and smiled at the painting of vivid, rapidly sketched figures in a Paris street, nodding. 'I like that one.' It had a gaiety and life she enjoyed.

'Klee was very prolific—and so was Picasso.' Gerard had moved on to stare at a drawing of a naked child, a few black lines scrawled on a sheet of paper. 'Picasso did so much work and was so easy to copy that it's almost impossible to tell when someone else has faked him. You need to be certain of the provenance. This looks genuine, though. You need to be a brilliant draughtsman to draw with such economy. If you look closely you can see that the artist never lifted his pen from the paper; he drew this fast, without stopping to think—that's what gives it this fluidity.'

'Are you an expert?' Keira asked drily.

He gave her another of his mocking little smiles. 'I have an arts degree; my special field is art of the twentieth century.'

She drew in her lower lip, angry with him—what else didn't she know about him? And why did she feel she should know everything there was to know? That was something she decided not to investigate—at least, not yet.

He turned away to look at some other paintings, then casually asked, 'Has your stepfather got any other pictures?'

Keira felt the hair on the back of her neck stand up. She intuitively knew they had reached the real reason why Gerard was here in Morocco.

'He has some in his private suite,' she said, watching Gerard.

'Which is locked.'

'Yes.'

'Do you have the key?'

'No.' His questions were too quick; she found herself biting out her replies, anger making her bristle.

'Does Hassan?'

'I have no idea.'

Hassan and Alima arrived with the coffee and cakes and Keira deliberately sat down on one of the brocade sofas, accepted a tiny cup of strong Arabic coffee, heavily sweetened, took a date and nut biscuit and nibbled it. Gerard sat down on a high-backed chair with a deeply upholstered red plush cushion on the seat, took coffee and a slice of the *fkoss*.

'What a very unusual flavour.'

'Caraway, poppy and aniseed,' Keira told him.

He lapsed into Arabic, from his smile congratulating Hassan on the bread. Hassan replied, smiling, and a few moments later left them alone. Alima withdrew too, but only into the hall, where she sat down on a bench, from which she could keep an eye on Keira and Gerard.

'Our chaperon,' Gerard drawled. 'I'm surprised you put up with it without complaint. I'd have expected you to get angry with him.'

'When in Rome...' muttered Keira. 'And I am only here for a week or so. Also I like Hassan. He's a nice guy.'

'How long has he worked for your stepfather?'

'Years.'

'He's very loyal to him?'

Keira gave him a suspicious look. 'Why? Planning to bribe him?'

He ignored the question, asking another of his own. 'Is your stepfather very rich?'

'Very,' she said through her teeth. 'What are you really doing here in Tangier, Mr Findlay? What are you up to? And don't tell me you followed me out here, because I don't buy that. You're more interested in my stepfather than you are in me. Why did you break in here last night? You came prepared to commit burglary, and obviously you knew the grounds were patrolled by dogs—why else would you have had that meat to hand?'

'I'm not a burglar or a thief, Keira,' he drawled.

She nodded. 'If you aren't, you took an almighty risk, climbing over the wall, carrying that assault equipment, the meat for the dog... If Hassan had caught you, he might have shot you, and I'm sure that thought had occurred to you. You're not stupid.'

'Thank you.' His grey eyes watched her coolly, appraisingly. 'Neither are you, obviously.'

She resented the veiled patronage and flared up. 'No, I'm not; don't make the mistake of thinking I am! I realise there's something behind all this and I want to know what it is—either you tell me or I call my stepfather and tell him there's a TV reporter sniffing around out here, and ask him what I ought to do about you. I think he'll tell me to call the police and have them deal with you—and I don't think they would treat you with kid gloves, not once I explained what you've been up to.'

'No, I don't imagine they would,' he said slowly, his mouth twisting into a cynical smile.

He finished his coffee and put the cup down on the low lacquered coffee-table in front of them. 'May I have some more coffee?'

The table was so low that she found it easier to kneel down to pour it, and when she turned to hand him the small cup she found him closer than he had been a few seconds ago. Startled, she looked up into his face, her breathing accelerating, her heart beating twice as fast.

He bent his head, whispered, 'We can't talk here; I'll explain later, when we're alone.'

Keira murmured something incoherently, appalled to find herself trembling. What they had been talking about vanished from her head. She could only think about the effect that her finding Gerard so close to her had had on her.

She scrambled back on to her feet and sat down again, face flushed, eyes lowered to hide from him the blinding rush of emotion that had swept through her. I mustn't fall in love with him—I can't; I couldn't bear the agony of that again, the piercing joy, the hope deferred, the terrible depressions at the end. Love hurts too much; only fools let themselves fall in love.

They left five minutes later, seen off by Hassan and Alima.

'I began to think they were going to insist on coming with us!' muttered Gerard as they drove away.

Keira had been afraid they might, too, but fortunately Hassan knew the hotel to which Gerard was taking her and he obviously felt she would be safe there.

The hotel was modern; white-walled, spacious and luxuriously furnished, it had a superb restaurant with both Arab and French chefs working in the kitchen and a dazzling menu.

Keira chose a chicken consommé in which floated tiny pieces of vegetable and chicken, following that with a baked local fish, served on a bed of salad and rice, without a sauce of any kind, although they offered her a bewildering variety, all of which she refused.

Gerard watched her eat only half the soup and less than half of the fish and refuse a pudding. As they left the table to go outside and drink their coffee on the hotel terrace, he asked her quietly, 'How long have you had an eating problem?'

She tensed, shrugging. 'Since my teens.' Her eyes lifted, fixed and angry. 'And I don't like talking about it.'

'I would have thought that was part of the therapy I gather you had to undergo? Talking always helps, whatever the problem, surely?'

'That depends on who you're talking to! It certainly doesn't include the media!'

He gave her a cool, level stare. 'How many times do I have to tell you? I'm not interested in doing a story on you.'

'Then why did you follow me to Tangier? You admit it isn't a coincidence! So why are you here?'

They walked out on to the canopied terrace overlooking the swimming-pool, and sat down in comfortable, cushioned basket-weave chairs. Gerard summoned the waiter, ordered coffee, then leaned back, crossing one long leg over the other, his lean body apparently very relaxed—but she noticed the way his hard eyes flicked around to make sure there was nobody else within earshot and the way his fingertips tapped restlessly on the side of his chair.

He was as calm as he wanted her to believe.

'Art,' he said quietly. 'I'm working on research about art thieves; they target big collectors, spend months getting all the background details, the security system, the servants, the dates when the owner is likely to be away—it's very professional. These people know exactly what they're doing.'

The sun was very hot by now, but they were sitting under a canvas awning, which flapped in the light breeze. Keira frowned, watching light dazzle and dance on the surface of the pool.

'And you suspect Ivo might be targeted by these people?'

'He's a big collector, I gather, although nothing I saw in the villa is valuable enough to attract this mob. That's why I asked if he had any other paintings not on view.'

'Why didn't you just approach Ivo, if you really suspect he might be burgled?'

'I have no proof he's on their list. I just happened to notice some very good paintings hanging on the walls in that photo I stole from you.'

'So that's why you stole it!'

'Partly,' he admitted, his eyes glinting. 'I wanted to check them out, make sure I wasn't imagining things. I have friends in the trade who know exactly where every famous work of art is, even in the most remote corners of the earth. This is a shrinking world, so far as art and antiques are concerned.'

She looked at him blankly. 'What are you talking about?'

The waiter brought their coffee; Gerard watched him pour it, offer cream and sugar, then bow and walk away. Only then did he answer her.

'People in Japan buy in London, people in Sydney buy in New York, people in Scotland buy in Tokyo. There are no longer any frontiers in art.' He took a sip from the tiny cup of very strong, sweet coffee. 'My friends looked at that photo and could tell me a great deal about the paintings—when they were last sold, who to and for how much. So, you see, there are, or were, some very valuable paintings in that room, which, I imagine, is the suite Hassan keeps locked?'

'That photo was taken in Ivo's suite,' she admitted flatly, having finished her coffee. 'But I don't know anything about the paintings he has there, although, of course, I've seen some of them. I've never really studied them, and he doesn't talk about them.'

She felt a knife twisting inside her. She had kept telling herself she didn't trust him, not to believe a word he said—but it hurt to face the fact that he had lied when he'd said he had come to Tangier to see her. She should have known better than to believe him.

Suddenly she had a sharp vision of him in her room last night, his powerful body naked, moving on top of her, the brush of his thigh against hers, the heat of his mouth as he kissed her. Her blood sang in her veins. She had to bite the inside of her mouth to stop a groan forcing itself out of her throat.

Desperate to hide her feelings, she jumped to her feet. 'I thought we were going to swim? Where do I change into my costume?'

He had made the suggestion just before they'd left the villa and Keira had gone up to her room to fetch a very demure one-piece costume, black with thin white piping and a flared ballet skirt covering her upper thighs. There was a kidney-shaped swimming-pool in the garden of the villa but she had not used it so far on this visit.

'You can do that in my room,' said Gerard and she stiffened, her colour rising.

'Aren't there any changing-rooms down here?'

He gave her a derisive look.

'I wasn't planning to get you upstairs and into bed! Don't worry, I won't come up with you. You can use my key; I'll wait until you get back then I'll go and change.'

He went to the desk and got his key, walked her to the row of lifts. 'Room 327 on the third floor. Turn right when you come out of the lift; it's about six rooms along on the left. I'll wait out on the terrace.'

She couldn't help being intensely curious as she opened the door of his room. It was only a room in a foreign hotel, where his stay would be very brief. He had only been there for a couple of days and wouldn't have much with him. Nevertheless there would be some trace of himself, even if only a book he was reading or the sort of aftershave he preferred!

The room had been cleaned by the hotel staff, so the bed was made and everything was very tidy. Keira picked up the two books on the bedside table: the latest thriller from Dick Francis and a paperback on modern art strewn with glossy reproductions. There was a folded sheet of paper acting as a bookmark between two of the photos of paintings. Keira looked first at the two pages; one painting was an abstract in violent reds and greens and yellows and the other was a haunting desert landscape with a foreground which held the skull of an animal, a scuttling spider, a snake and the black shadow of the only tree in the landscape, a eucalyptus, the slender, graceful outline unmistakable before you noticed the smooth grey bark peeling off in orange-coloured strips.

She felt an immediate leap of recognition; there was no question but that she had seen that painting before—in Ivo's suite, hanging on the wall of his enormous bedroom.

She read the caption but didn't recognise the name of the Australian artist. What did startle her was to read that the painting was the property of a museum in Texas. Had Ivo bought it from them? Museums don't generally sell off anything from their collection, surely? It was more likely that Ivo had a copy.

Does he know the picture is only a copy, though? Keira wondered, shutting the book again. As she did so, the folded piece of paper Gerard had been using as a bookmark fluttered to the ground. Bending, she picked it up and was about to replace it when she caught sight of her own name written on one side of it.

She had to find out what he had written about her. She unfolded the paper; it turned out to be a piece of pale yellow copy paper with a few hurriedly handwritten notes on it. Her eye skimmed over the lines.

Had Gerard written the words? She had never seen his handwriting, so she couldn't tell, but someone had jotted down her name—followed by a stream of questions. 'Keira... Aware of what's going on? Innocent? What about Krensky? Which side of the fence? How dangerous? Back-up?'

She stared at the notes, her brows knit in bewilderment and a sense of creeping dismay. What on earth did it mean? One thing was certain. Gerard wasn't telling her everything.

She carefully refolded the paper and put it back in the book, put the book back on his bedside table, then began to get changed in a hurry, in his bathroom, with the door locked.

When she had put on the smooth-fitting swimsuit she pushed her hair into the white bathing cap which matched it, then assessed her reflection a little uncertainly.

The swimsuit might have seemed demure back in London, but somehow the way it clung to every curve of her body made her suddenly uneasy about going down to the public swimming-pool in it. She should have brought a beach robe with her. She looked round the bathroom, hoping to see one hanging behind the door, as you often saw in modern luxury hotels, but there were only towels on display, soft, fluffy white towels in a generous heap.

Sighing, she unlocked the door to step out and stopped dead in her tracks.

Gerard was in the bedroom. For a heart-stopping second she thought he was naked. She was so shaken that she didn't even scream, she just stared, eyes stretched as far as they would go, her body beginning to tremble violently. She took in his bare, tanned flesh, roughened on the chest and arms by short, curling black hair, absorbed the fact that his long, long legs were bare too, and felt her breathing quicken, her face flush hotly.

Only as an after-flash did she realise that he was not, in fact, naked. He was wearing black swimming trunks.

Had she wanted to see him naked so much that she had simply blotted out the fact that he wasn't actually nude? What was happening to her? Desire turned into self-contempt and rage, a flashpoint which made her snap at him, 'What are you doing in here? How did you get in? You said you'd wait for me downstairs.'

'I was going to,' he said coolly, 'then I remembered I was expecting an important phone call at three o'clock and I was afraid that if I wasn't in my room I'd miss it; the operators here aren't very good at tracking you down if you aren't in your room. So I asked the floor housekeeper to let me in with the service key.'

She wasn't placated. Angrily she demanded, 'Why didn't you knock on the door and ask me if it was OK?'

'I did knock,' he told her curtly, her aggression fuelling an answering anger in him.

'I don't believe you!'

His face hardened. 'Don't call me a liar, Keira! I did knock, even if you didn't hear me.'

She gave him a blistering look of disbelief. 'And why did you start taking your clothes off while I was still here? I could have walked out of the bathroom at any minute.'

His eyes gleamed insolently between those dark lashes. 'You've seen me naked before. Last night.'

'You should have banged on the bathroom door before you started undressing; you should have warned me!' She turned on her heel. 'I'll go down to the pool while you wait for your telephone call.'

He stepped between her and the door. 'What is your problem, Keira?'

'You, at the moment! Will you stop hassling me?'

'Don't be flip. I was serious—you must have some emotional hang-up or you wouldn't be bulimic. I didn't really know what that meant until I talked to a doctor friend. He explained that it wasn't greed, it was the very opposite—a pathologically insatiable hunger.'

She stood, frozen in pain, her eyes fixed on the floor.

'Is that a fair description, Keira?' His voice was gentle, but she still didn't trust him.

'I don't want to talk about it. Mind your own business.'

'Maybe if you talked about it you wouldn't have a problem. Why are you so suspicious of men? Did something happen when you were a child? Did you have an unhappy childhood?'

She looked at him scornfully. 'You do love the obvious, don't you?'

'I'm groping in the dark here, Keira. You might help me. At least tell me why you're so hostile. What have I done to deserve the way you talk to me?'

'You mean apart from forcing your attentions on me in my own home? Turning up in the middle of the night dressed as a burglar, scaling my walls and breaking into my bedroom, taking off all your clothes and jumping on me?'

'It wasn't like that!'

'Oh, yes, it was! I certainly didn't send you an invitation.'

He angrily grimaced. 'I thought you would be asleep.'

Rage almost shot through the top of her head. 'Oh, sorry to have disappointed you. What if I had been? What was on the agenda? Rape?'

His jaw tightened, his eyes like chips of grey stone. 'Is that what you really think of me? That I'm that sort of bastard?'

She hesitated briefly, realising that, in fact, she didn't—she had been so angry she had flung words at him without meaning all of them.

'Just because I'm a model it doesn't mean I'm available to any man I meet!' she said at last.

'I've never given you the impression that I think you are!' he told her furiously. 'And I resent being classed with the sort of guy who thinks that way.'

Her green eyes smouldered. 'Oh, well, then, I must have hallucinated what happened in my bedroom last night!'

There was an odd, tense silence, then he said softly, 'That wasn't a casual pass, Keira.' His gaze moved down over her body in the tight-fitting costume. Her pulses accelerated as she took in the dark flush moving under his skin, the sound of his quickening breath.

'Get out of my way,' she whispered in a voice that shook.

He moved, but only to come closer. 'You know it meant more than that for both of us, Keira.'

'Leave me alone!'

'If you meant that you wouldn't look at me the way you did just now,' he said softly, and she was stricken, her skin turning first white, then red.

He knew. He had picked up on the desire which had pierced her when she'd walked out of the bathroom and seen him standing there, almost naked. Shame made her face burn. She couldn't get a sound out. She just wished the floor would open up and swallow her.

'You want me as much as I want you, Keira,' he murmured, and his hand lifted, dragged the white cap from her head; her red hair came tumbling down in waves like the sea, curling strands as light as air, floating around her face. He caught hold of some of the strands, watched as they coiled around his fingers, living springs, fine and golden red.

'Don't——!' she began, but couldn't finish because how could she say to him, Don't touch me because I want it too much, don't make me fall in love with you, don't send me crazy with passion, don't walk away and leave me to die of misery? He mustn't guess she was balanced on a tightrope over a chasm of love so deep that it was unfathomable, no love could ever be enough to fill it, she would be empty and aching for the rest of her life.

Gerard wasn't listening to her; he was absorbed in his own reactions, playing with her hair and staring at it with eyes that glittered. 'You look like one of those Pre-Raphaelite girls,' he murmured thickly. 'They always have hair like this, like some living thing. Funny stuff, hair, especially women's hair. Leonardo da Vinci was always drawing long, curling hair; sometimes his drawings of hair turn into swirls of water, cascades of it. Your hair looks like fire . . . orange and red tongues of flame.'

His hand slid slowly through her hair, downwards, stroking her scalp, the nape of her neck, down over her silky bare shoulders.

'Stop it,' she muttered, shuddering in tortured, unwilling pleasure. The brush of his hand was so light, so delicate, an exquisite pain.

A second later she felt his fingers drift further down, slip between the taut cup of her swimsuit bra and her flesh, and her nipples grew hot and hardened.

She had to get away before her desire ran out of control; her defences would start crashing down any second. Desperately, she tried to dart past him but Gerard caught her, swung her round to face him, her back pushed against the door.

'No!' she cried out, her green eyes wide and wild.

Before she could move again his body held her captive, one leg pushed between hers, nudging them apart, his bare chest warm-fleshed on her, and then his mouth searched down her cheek, found her lips and parted them hungrily. She fought not to give in to the wild quivering desire running through her; she turned her head this way and that like a trapped animal, half suffocated by his mouth, until Gerard cupped her throat with one hand, pushing her head back so that she couldn't move it.

She gave a high gasp as he pulled the thin straps of her swimsuit down.

'No!'

He was staring down at her breasts, the warm flesh rounding and lifting in excitement, the nipples standing out, pink and hard.

Gerard bent his head. His tongue stroked sensuously and she gave a strangled moan of pleasure, her knees almost giving way. He lifted his head to look down at her, his eyes half hooded, glittering darkly behind his black lashes, his gaze brooding on her face. What was he thinking? she wondered, staring back at him, feeling dizzy and weak as she looked deep into those compelling grey eyes. It was like looking into the heart of night, being swallowed into darkness.

'Keira...' He said her name in deep, hoarse syllables, as if it was an invocation.

She closed her eyes helplessly, her ears deafened by the beating of her own blood through her veins. His mouth was on hers a second later. She abandoned herself to the heated movements of his mouth, her body trembling against him.

Gerard lifted her off her feet, without taking his mouth off hers, and carried her across the room to the bed.

CHAPTER SIX

IT WAS only when Gerard lowered her to the yielding bed, his mouth reluctantly lifting from hers, that Keira could breathe and think again, and realised how it was going to end unless she did something to stop him, and did it quickly.

She jackknifed up, shaking her head, panic beating inside her because she didn't know him well enough to be sure how he would react if she tried to say no now. After all, she hadn't been fighting him off; she had been kissing him back with every sign of passion and she was already half naked.

Some men in this situation would refuse to take no for an answer. What would she do if he turned nasty? If he tried to use force?

'What the hell's wrong? You can't stop now,' he groaned, trying to pull her down again.

Why did I agree to come up here to his room? she thought desperately as she saw his glittering eyes and darkly flushed face, heard the ragged intake of his breathing.

I trusted him! she argued with herself in her own defence. He gave me the key and said he would wait downstairs.

But you shouldn't have trusted him! she thought with bitterness. He's a man, isn't he? You should have known this was on the cards.

'You know you want me as much as I want you, Keira!' he said, and it was true; she did.

She wanted him far more than he wanted her, in fact—although she certainly wasn't going to tell him so. Her whole body was aching with the desire to take him into itself and have him become part of her. Her heart ached with the need to love him, to let the dammed-up passion of her life flood out into him: the intensity of her feelings terrified her. Love was too important to her, meant too much. She had an insatiable need for it. What had he said to her earlier? That she had an insatiable hunger for food? He hadn't mentioned love, but since her bulimia had been diagnosed Keira had seen too many psychoanalysts, had endured their questions, their probing, their talk of the unconscious and its symbolism, not to know that food could be a substitute for love.

She might understand the root of her problems, but that didn't automatically cure them. The black anguish at the very base of her memory might be poisoning her mind, but how did you reach it and end the pain?

Until she was cured of this endless tangle of need and rejection, love was always going to give her pain.

What if I already love him? she thought in a painful spasm of honesty, and nausea rose in her throat.

She put her hand to her mouth. 'I'm going to be sick!' she gasped, and Gerard shifted away in shocked surprise. Stumbling off the bed, she ran for the bathroom without looking back.

Behind her as she slammed the door she heard a stunned silence. She turned on both taps in the bathroom sink before she threw up; she did not want him to hear her.

Afterwards she washed her face in cold water for a long time, but her reflection still showed her a pale face and reddened eyes. She looked at herself with bitter contempt. Your head is in a mess! she told herself. Isn't it time you unscrambled whatever brains you have left?

While she was drying her face she heard the telephone begin to ring, then Gerard's terse, deep voice talking. Keira no longer felt she could bear to swim; she got dressed again and then sat down on the edge of the bath waiting for Gerard to ring off.

She caught snatches of the conversation. 'Not yet. I haven't had a chance. I think we may be right, but until I actually see the canvas how can I be sure? If it's a copy I'll know, but I must spend some time with the picture, and I can't get in there.' A brief silence then he said impatiently, 'Because it's kept locked!' Keira's heart skipped. Even paler, she stood up, moved silently to the door and leaned her ear against the thin panels.

'No, I can't break in,' Gerard said. 'I don't want to end up in prison here; Moroccan prisons aren't holiday camps.'

What was this all about? she wondered, biting her lip. Whatever he was up to it was far more complicated than he had wanted her to believe.

Another silence followed, then he said, 'I'm working on it, but it will take time and patience. OK, Todd, I'll keep in touch.'

She heard the phone go down. She would wait a moment or two and then come out; she didn't want him to know she had been eavesdropping.

She didn't hear him move, but suddenly his voice said curtly on the other side of the door, 'You can come out now, Keira.'

She started in shock. He knew she had been listening. She slowly opened the door and looked at him almost with the same shock she had felt when she'd come out of the bathroom a quarter of an hour ago and thought for a second that he was naked. She knew now that he wasn't—but she still got a jab of bitter desire as she saw the smooth, wide shoulders, the bare, muscled chest, those long, dark-haired legs.

'You heard all that,' Gerard said coolly, his glance flicking from head to foot and absorbing the fact that she had got dressed again. She saw his mouth indent in sardonic comment.

Keira's green eyes threw back defiance at him. 'Yes,' she snapped. 'And I want to know what you were talking about or I really will ring my stepfather.'

He nodded, gesturing to a chair by the window. 'I was going to talk to you anyway. Sit down.'

She was still trembling, a pulse beating in her throat; she was afraid of being alone with him in this room while he was almost naked. She took a deep breath and managed to walk steadily to the high-backed, black-lacquered chair and sit down, then, without looking at him, she muttered, 'Would you get dressed first, please? In the bathroom.'

He said something explosive under his breath, then bit out, 'If you give me your word you won't run off while I'm in there!'

She nodded, still with bent head. 'I promise.'

He strode to the wardrobe, began opening doors, pulling out clean clothes, then he went into the bathroom, banging the door after him. She looked out of the window at the hot blue sky, saw the ragged edge of palm leaves clawing at the horizon, heard children's voices and the splash as they jumped into the swimming-pool in the hotel grounds.

Tears pricked at her eyes. She had come very close to losing control a few minutes ago. If she had, she would be hating herself now. Hating him, too.

Liar, said the little voice in her head. You don't hate him. You're already in love with him.

Every last trace of colour left her face. Don't even let yourself think it! she told herself furiously. Desire isn't love; it's just an instinct you can't control. Love is ten times worse, and you mustn't let yourself love Gerard Findlay. White and drawn, she ran the back of her hand angrily across her face, rubbing out the tears before he could see the traces of them.

The bathroom opened and she started violently, her head swinging round, her wild red hair flying around her white face. He had put on sand-coloured jeans and an open-necked white shirt; she should have been relieved to see him fully clothed but instead all she could think was that he looked intensely sexy in the jeans.

Gerard gave her a dry, sardonic stare. 'OK. I've got my clothes back on; you can relax. The explosive is defused.'

A stain of bright red appeared in her cheeks. She looked away again, a little muscle twitching beside her mouth.

'That is how you see me, isn't it?' he drawled. 'You're afraid I might blow you sky-high if you're not careful.'

Her breath caught. He was far too close to the truth. She was terrified of what else he might guess. Hurriedly she asked, 'Who were you talking to on the phone? You were being told to break into my stepfather's suite, weren't you? Why?'

He walked over to the bed and sat down on the edge of it. 'I told you, I'm working on a story about an art smuggling ring. And your stepfather is a collector.' He paused then asked her, 'How do you get on with him, by the way? Are you very fond of him? Is he fond of you?'

She laughed with bitterness, her eyes an angry green. 'I remind him that my mother was married before. He's a jealous, possessive man; he hates to hear my father mentioned, he never wanted me around when I was younger, and I was sent away to school to get rid of me—he resents my very existence and always has.'

Gerard watched her closely, frowning. 'And how do you feel about him?'

She turned her suspicious, distrustful eyes on him. 'You're always asking me questions but you never tell me anything about yourself!'

'What do you want to know?' he promptly asked her, shifting on the bed, his lean body casually graceful in every move he made.

She averted her gaze, heat burning inside her. Desire prickled constantly every time he moved. She

forced herself to think instead, to use her head and
ignore the clamouring of her body. 'Are your
parents still alive?'

'Yes, both of them—they live in Cornwall, in a
doll's-house cottage on the quayside of a little
village on the coast. My father was born there; he
went to London to become a reporter on a Fleet
Street newspaper but he retired five years ago and
finally managed to achieve his dream of going home
to Cornwall. He's a big man, gone grey now, but
still pretty tough. My mother doesn't look tough—
in fact she's like a bouncy rubber ball, round and
soft and full of energy—but she's as tough as blazes
underneath. She had to be—she taught in London
schools for years, and life doesn't come much
tougher than that. Some of her kids were mini ter-
rorists, out to commit mayhem in the classroom.
Mum had a dream of living beside the sea too. Now
she and my father spend all their time either gar-
dening, going on country walks or fishing in their
own little boat, and they're blissfully happy.'

'They sound nice,' she said, her delicate face
wistful, not merely because his parents sounded
wonderful but because of the obvious affection with
which he talked about them.

'They are,' he said gently, hearing the note of
envy in her voice. Families could be the devil, he
thought. Had she been starved of love at home?
Unwanted by her stepfather... and what about her
real father? What part had he played in her life?
He was increasingly curious about her. She was such
a frail, almost fragile creature; she weighed very
little more than a child and yet her slender body
had a sexual allure that made him ache to touch

her every time he saw her. She needed to be protected, cared for—he had a feeling nobody ever had looked after her and he wanted to do it.

He had never felt this way before, but then he had never before met a woman who looked like a lost child and a siren all at the same time. He wanted to hold her in his arms until she stopped looking sad and haunted and started to look happy. He wondered if she ever had, and thought cynically that if he had her in his arms he would stop thinking of her as a child and start making love to her; he wouldn't be able to help himself. She turned him on more than any woman he had ever seen.

'Do you have brothers or sisters?' Keira asked and he nodded.

'A sister, three years younger than me.'

'Does she look like you?'

He looked surprised, then laughed. 'There's a very faint family resemblance, I suppose. Janet's got my colouring, but she inherited her physical build from my mother. She's married, to a dentist, and they have a couple of kids and live in Devon, so they're able to see a lot of my parents.'

'Do you see a lot of them?'

'If I'm in Britain I do—sometimes I don't get to see them for months, if I'm working overseas.'

'Do you miss them when you haven't seen them for ages?' She was deeply curious about his feelings; she wanted to get inside his head and know him as well as she knew herself, although that was impossible and ridiculous; you could never know another human being as well as you knew yourself. Telling herself that didn't stop her wanting to find out everything she could about him, though.

He nodded. 'We talk on the phone, and I send them postcards—there's never time to write letters when you're working in a war zone! But I start to miss them if I don't actually see them for months.'

'And they miss you? They must worry about you when you're out there, somewhere dangerous?'

He smiled crookedly. 'They do, of course. My mother worries the most—my father doesn't say much but I expect he does too. But he's a reporter himself, he knows the job, and he knows I take care not to risk my life unless it's absolutely necessary.'

She felt a stab of agony as she realised how dangerous his job was—one day he might be killed on one of these assignments overseas.

'They must have been scared when you were so badly injured on your last assignment!'

'I was in the wrong place at the wrong time, and at least I came out alive. A lot of people didn't, including women and children.'

She looked at him with sombre, shadowed eyes. 'I remember seeing the report on TV.' At the time she had only felt a faint shock at the thought of someone she knew being involved in the fighting over there. From now on she knew it would be a nightmare for her every time he was abroad on a foreign story.

'It's a dangerous job,' she said aloud, her eyes burning on his face. He was too dangerous to love. She would be crazy to let herself fall for him; the risk of getting hurt was far too high.

Oh, come on! the bleak little voice in her head mocked. You know it's too late to use words like 'if'. You're past the stage of being able to stop yourself. Admit it. You're mad about him; you've had him on your mind for months. You always knew you could fall for him, right from the first day you saw him, and now you have, even if you won't admit it.

She was trembling, her lids down over the green eyes turned cloudy with sensuality and yearning.

He watched her, his pulses beating fast at the sight of the parted, quivering line of her pink mouth, the vulnerable fragility of her pale throat, those long, dark lashes fluttering against her cheek. She was breathtaking, he thought. He had thought her beautiful the first time he'd seen her, but the word didn't even begin to cover it. What was going on behind the delicate, shadowed lids? What was she thinking? Feeling?

He had to know. He wanted to know everything about her. 'Now you know all there is to know about me, what about you, Keira? I asked you how you felt about your stepfather; you didn't tell me.'

'I don't like him,' she confessed abstractedly because she was still so wrapped up in the realisation of just how much she cared for him. It was no secret, anyway; Sara could tell him, if he asked; Sara knew how she felt about Ivo.

Gerard went on watching her. 'Tell me about him.'

'I don't really want to talk about it.'

'I told you about my family.'

She grimaced. 'Your family love you and you love them. It isn't the same.'

'Tell me about that, then.'

She wanted to. Badly. And she was afraid to. Afraid because if she once started to trust him that much she would tell him everything and reveal herself, expose herself to his curious eyes. He would know too much about her, he would understand the dammed-up need for love which dominated everything she did and felt, and he would be scared off. Men found intensity disturbing.

Her nervous eyes flickered to him and away. Gerard stood up, walked over to the window and sat down on the edge of the windowsill, very close to her.

Her pulses leapt at his nearness like candle-flames in a high wind. For a second she couldn't breathe.

'Tell me, Keira,' he said in a quiet voice, his eyes hypnotic in their fixed gaze.

She looked down, fighting to breathe normally again. After a minute, she said, 'I didn't like Ivo from the minute I first set eyes on him. With my father gone and Ivo as my stepfather I no longer had a home—not that I ever really had one. My mother isn't the maternal type. She hated having a baby; I think she had a lot of pain during childbirth.'

'Women do, though, don't they?' Gerard said curtly. 'It doesn't stop them having other babies.'

She smiled drily. 'I think they forget between babies what it's like, and then, when they get the first labour pains, they think, Oh, no! I remember now; why did I let this happen again? But by then it's too late. My mother says she nearly died; I don't know how true that is—but I do know that after she'd had me she told my father there wouldn't be another child and he wanted a son. I think their marriage never had a chance after that.'

'Is that why your parents divorced? Just because she wouldn't have another baby?' To Gerard they sounded like a thoroughly selfish pair, neither of them concerned about the child they'd brought into the world, only interested in themselves.

'I don't know the full story, I only know my mother's side of it. They quarrelled all the time, though; I do remember that. I'm not even sure whether they split up over Ivo or my mother met Ivo later. It all happened too fast. My father went away, and then Ivo appeared. My mother says there was no problem over custody of me—my father didn't want me anyway; he didn't contest custody.'

Gerard frowned angrily. 'She told you that? My God, didn't she realise how that would hurt you? It sounds as if she was taking her revenge on him by making sure you grew up hating him.'

'You're wrong—my mother isn't vindictive and she doesn't hate my father. She's simply indifferent. She has always talked to me as if I'm grown-up, but she prefers to think of me as a girlfriend—not a daughter. I've never been allowed to call her Mother; I've always been told to use her first name. When I was in my teens, I rather liked that; it made me feel grown-up. Having a child ages you, she says. It makes people think about your age, whereas if you don't have a child you're as young as you look. To be fair to her, she didn't intend to hurt me, and she didn't tell me anything I didn't know about my father; I remembered him well enough to know that I didn't count much with him. If I'd been a boy he might have been more interested, but as I was a girl...well, he wasn't unkind or unpleasant, he was just busy and indifferent.' She paused, then said drily, 'They both were.'

Gerard was silent, thinking over what she had said, and she watched him with anxiety, wishing she hadn't been so frank, hoping he wasn't reading between the lines, guessing too much.

'In a sense you didn't have parents at all, did you?' he finally said, and she stared at him, green eyes wide open in reaction to the question. Gerard stared back, his face unreadable. 'Neither of them loved you or cared about you—that's how it sounds. They weren't cruel, they just didn't love you.'

She didn't answer because to speak might have been to burst into tears. She fought to keep herself under control, her body tense and locked, her mind locked too, desperate not to betray anything else to him.

As if he picked up on her feelings, Gerard turned and stared out of the window; she could only see his profile, hard-edged, frowning.

Then he started talking in a quiet, low-key way. 'I'm investigating a staggering increase in the theft of valuable paintings and sculpture. My colleague, who's our arts correspondent, and who has been working on this story for months, believes the thefts are carefully planned and orchestrated by someone who already has a buyer in mind before the crime is ever committed. In other words, they steal to order.'

She frowned. 'Where does Ivo fit in? You don't think he's the boss of this ring?' Oddly she didn't find the idea laughable; he certainly had no moral scruples that she had ever observed. He was a materialistic, grasping, selfish man who would think nothing of breaking the law if it suited him and made him richer, and it would also explain his strangely cloudy background, the past he was so reluctant to talk about, how he had made his money and where he came from.

Gerard was watching her closely, his grey eyes narrowed and sharp. 'No, my colleague has some idea who that might be, and it certainly isn't Ivo Krensky. But your stepfather may have bought paintings from these people.'

'Knowing them to be stolen?'

'Possibly even having ordered them,' said Gerard.

'The Australian painting I saw in that book,' she thought aloud, glancing at the book lying on his bedside table.

'Exactly.' He walked over and picked the book up, brought it back to her, opened at the glossy reproduction she had seen earlier. 'He does have it, doesn't he?'

She nodded. 'In the suite.'

'It was one of these I recognised in the photograph I stole from you. That was why I spoke to Todd about Krensky...'

'Todd?'

'My colleague. He knew the name immediately—your stepfather is a noted collector and Todd wasn't surprised by the idea that he might be somehow involved in the ring. His name had come up elsewhere, but he wasn't one of the leading figures; Todd hadn't been investigating him.'

'So he asked you to?'

'He suggested I might check out the painting in the photo—after all, it might be a copy.'

'I doubt it,' she said honestly. 'Ivo doesn't have copies in his collection in the suite. In fact, he doesn't have copies, full stop. He always says he would rather have a painting by an unknown that he can pick up for a song in a backstreet gallery, but which is at least an original, than a copy, however good, of a famous work by a great master.'

'Then if that painting is genuine it was stolen, and he probably knows it.'

She was sure he was right. She didn't like Ivo, but she respected his opinions on art—he knew what he was talking about. She had often wondered why he hadn't gone in for a career in art, but then he probably wouldn't have earned the sort of money that would make it possible for him to own valuable paintings, and Ivo hungered to own the beautiful things he worshipped. It wasn't enough for him to love a painting—he had to possess it. And one good picture would never have been enough. He wanted rooms full of them.

Yes, Ivo would know exactly what that painting was and where it came from; he had to be aware it had been stolen.

Gerard still watched her face. 'I'm right, aren't I?' he quietly insisted. 'He knows it's stolen.'

She met his eyes without answering. She didn't quite know what to say—she didn't like Ivo, but he was her mother's husband and he had been generous to Keira, rather reluctantly perhaps, but nevertheless he had been free with money where she was concerned. He had paid for her expensive schooling—happy to do it if it meant she was kept out of his way. He had offered her the mews cottage in Chelsea rent-free—for the same reason. If she was living in London in her own little place she was not living with him and her mother. Ivo would rather she didn't exist at all, but given that she did he was ready to pay to keep her at a distance. Keira hadn't accepted his offer; she paid him a monthly rent for the cottage, but she knew it was pegged below the market price he could get. She could have looked for somewhere else, but she knew it eased her mother's conscience to know that Keira was living in a place Ivo owned.

'You don't need to answer that,' Gerard murmured, his mouth wry. 'I shouldn't have asked.'

She lifted her chin and looked him straight in the eye. 'No, you shouldn't. I'm not shopping my stepfather; even if I knew for sure that he was involved, I couldn't possibly tell you. My mother would never forgive me.'

'You're fond of her, even if she doesn't want to admit you're her daughter?'

She held her expression steady, furious with herself for having told him so much.

All these years she had locked her secrets away, refused to let anyone—except the analysts at the clinic her stepfather had made her visit—glimpse her emotional turmoil, the constant battle between her agonising need for love and her fear of it, and now she had freely given herself away to his man without considering what use he might make of what he had learnt.

He was a reporter, after all; he earned his living by selling other people's secrets, by investigating and probing and exposing people.

How could I be so stupid? she thought.

'She's my mother,' she said defiantly. 'It may be old-fashioned but I believe in family loyalty.'

'Even if it isn't mutual?'

'You can't put conditions on it. Family is family. Any disagreement I might have with my mother is private, nothing to do with anyone else, especially not a TV reporter.'

'OK, I won't ask you anything else—but will you do just one thing for me?'

'What?' she asked warily.

'Get me into your stepfather's private suite so that I can see that painting and decide whether or not it's genuine or a copy.'

CHAPTER SEVEN

GERARD drove her back to the villa ten minutes later, avoiding the busy, crowded, modern part of Tangier, with its shops and offices and factories, not to mention the traffic jams of cars and vans and lorries that accompanied modern living. Instead he followed the coast road and minor, less cluttered roads, until he turned inland. It wasn't long before they were driving through open countryside, green at first but then scrubby and rough terrain with sandy soil and gorse and thorn trees. In the distance they saw the peaks of the Atlas mountains like sandy clouds floating in the brilliant blue sky. It was wellnigh impossible to guess how close they were—the eye was easily deceived, as Keira knew. The mountains could be a hundred miles away—or ten.

Neither she nor Gerard spoke much. She was worrying about what he had told her, about the possible consequences for Ivo and therefore for her mother—she had no idea what Gerard was thinking, but his profile was tense, moody. He stared straight ahead, driving very fast, faster than she thought wise on this narrow, winding road. He had to brake hard when they almost ran into a man on a camel; the car skidded on the sandy road and the camel gave an ear-splitting shriek and plunged forward wildly, going into hyperdrive, the rider furiously trying to rein it in, beating it with the stick he carried.

Gerard's wheels spun and his hands moved fast on the wheel as he got the car back under control, swearing softly under his breath. He pulled into the side of the road and sat there for a minute, frowning up at the hot blue sky, his whole body tense.

'You were driving too fast,' Keira began, and he turned his dark head and glared, snapping at her,

'I'm well aware of that. Don't give me lectures.'

'Don't take it out on me! It wasn't my fault you almost killed that camel.'

His face tightened even more, he snarled, 'It was your fault I was in a temper.'

'Don't you shout at me! If you're in a bad temper it's because you hate not getting your own way. You should never have asked me to get you into Ivo's suite. Now will you get this car back on the road and get me back to the villa?'

He gave her another glare, his grey eyes glittering, put his foot down hard on the accelerator and shot away. Luckily they did not run into any more camels although they almost made a small man in a grey djellabah fall off his donkey. He shouted after them, clenching his fist. Gerard made apologetic signals out of the open window.

Keira looked back as they drove on, saying scathingly, 'Next time maybe you'll succeed in killing someone!'

The sarcasm made Gerard glower morosely at her. 'At least I don't try to kill myself!'

She caught her breath, wincing. 'Neither do I! I know Sara told you my... my problem... could be life-threatening, but that's pretty rare and... and anyway I'm getting better all the time. That lapse in London was down to sudden shock. I haven't had another slip; I'm back under control.' She took a deep breath then said fiercely, 'I am not suicidal. I may have been once, but not any more.'

He was silent for a minute, driving with a frown carved into his forehead, then said roughly, 'I'm sorry. I shouldn't have said that.'

'No, you shouldn't!' But her voice no longer held rage. His apology had softened her.

He slowed as they approached the locked gates of the villa. Pulling up in front of them, Gerard spoke, in Arabic, into the electronic surveillance system, and Hassan's voice crackled back from the box high on the wall. The gates slowly swung open and Gerard drove through them. The car moved at a pace of about five miles an hour.

The late afternoon sun gleamed on the fig trees, the flame trees and rough-barked palms, the thick green leaves of magnolia trees. After the heat of the day the garden was full of rich, exotic scents.

His hands resting on the wheel, Gerard turned his head and looked at her briefly but searchingly.

'I apologize for asking you to help me nail your stepfather, Keira. It was selfish and stupid of me. Of course you can't. Whatever your relationship with him, I realise you would never do anything to hurt your mother—that's it, isn't it?' He pulled up outside the villa, switched off the engine and turned to face her.

She nodded, her mouth quivering. He touched her cheek with one finger and she felt her body leap with awareness of him.

'I'm getting to know you very well,' he murmured, and her breath caught. She couldn't meet his eyes for fear of what she might betray. She could have told him that she was getting to know him too; she was beginning to recognise every fleeting expression passing over his face, every nuance in his voice. She certainly felt the physical instincts moving in his body now. The air between them vibrated with a desire that made her weak.

They sat there in silence for a minute, their breathing rapid, then Gerard gave a long sigh before asking her abruptly, 'Are you going to warn him?'

'Yes,' she said, and then her green eyes lifted to stare back at him. She had known she must ever since she'd understood exactly what the situation was and how much of a threat it would mean to Ivo and, more importantly, to her mother.

Frowning, Gerard said, 'He's as much a criminal as the men who actually stole the pictures, you know.'

'Yes.' She wasn't going to dispute that, or pretend she didn't disapprove of Ivo.

Impatiently, Gerard protested, 'And he's rich; he could afford to buy most things he wants, so long as they're on the open market. He couldn't have bought the Australian picture because it was hanging in a public gallery, and in my book that's what damns him—because it was there for all of us to see and now it isn't; now it's hidden away for a rich man to gloat over on his own.'

'I know.' Ivo's behaviour was unforgivable, but she wasn't offering him forgiveness, she was simply acting out of family loyalty.

One part of her mind told her she was a fool, pointed out that Ivo undoubtedly felt no loyalty to her, and had never shown her any family affection—but she had to protect her mother, and that meant giving Ivo a chance to save himself, if he could.

Gerard's frown deepened. 'You can't approve of that! It's pure greed, the worst sort of selfishness. He can have anything he wants and can buy legally, but he gets more of a kick out of stolen property. I'm prepared to bet he enjoys his "secret" paintings more than those he has hanging where anyone who visits his house can see them.'

She gave a little sigh, nodding. 'I'm sure he does.' She had often seen Ivo come out of his suite looking like a cat that had stolen cream, a strange, gloating self-satisfaction on his face.

Gerard said flatly, 'Men like him love to lock beautiful things away, keep them hidden, enjoy them on their own. And living here in Tangier there isn't the same risk as there is in Europe of the stolen art division of Interpol getting on to him.'

'But now you've tracked him down,' she said huskily. 'Through me.'

He fixed his narrowed eyes on her face. 'You feel guilty? Is that why you feel you have to tell him? That's stupid. You had no idea about all this and you didn't tell me anything—I simply saw a photo in your bedroom and recognised a painting I was sure had been stolen. It was pure luck.'

'Bad luck for Ivo,' she said on a grimace. 'And he's going to blame me for it. It may not be my fault, but it happened because of me, and Ivo will suspect I told you more than I actually did.' Would

Ivo be far wrong, though? She had told Gerard a great deal—she had said far more than she should have done. She hadn't told Gerard she believed Ivo to be involved in this art racket, but she had helped him to fill in blanks in the picture he had of Ivo's activities and background, so, in a sense, she had helped Ivo's enemies, and that was undoubtedly how he would see it.

'He'll blame me,' she repeated with a faint sigh.

'Don't tell him, then,' Gerard said curtly.

'I have to. You know that. He has to be warned that he's being investigated.'

'Why? All that will do is give him time to hide the evidence, and those paintings should go back where they belong, not be squirrelled away again, somewhere even more remote, by Krensky. He has no right to them. They belong to all of us, not one rich man.'

She sighed, recognising the truth of that, and torn between her family duty and her sense of right and wrong.

'If you are going to warn him I'll have to call Interpol and tell them I suspect the paintings are here!' Gerard bit out.

'Don't try to blackmail or bully me! It won't work. You must do whatever you think is right. So will I.' She got out of the car just as Hassan appeared at the front door, his face serious, unsmiling. She slammed the car door and Gerard started the engine and drove off with a roar of acceleration. Hassan stared after him, then switched his frowning stare to Keira's face. She saw disapproval in his expression.

'Mr Krensky rang while you were out this afternoon, Miss Keira.'

She stiffened, her lips parting in an audible intake of air. 'Did he want to speak to me?'

'No, he rang to talk to me about his plans for the next few months, but while we were talking he did ask if you were enjoying your visit. He had asked me to take care of you while you were here, so I told him about Mr Findlay coming here, and he seemed surprised.'

Keira felt her nerves prickle. I bet he was surprised, she thought grimly.

'The master knew who he was, but he said he did not know that you knew Mr Findlay.' Hassan's face held reproach, veiled accusation. She had deliberately let him think that Ivo and her mother knew that Gerard was staying in Tangier. She had allowed Hassan to believe that she and Gerard were going to be married and that her family approved.

Hassan's accusing eyes said that she had deliberately deceived him.

Keira's chin lifted defiantly. 'I'll talk to him myself—I was going to ring Florida anyway.' She didn't bother to retort that she was not a child, she was a modern woman with a life of her own who did not need to ask permission before she went out with the man of her choice. She knew Hassan would not be happy with that, however true it might be. This was his city, his culture and lifestyle, and her attitudes clashed with his; they upset and disturbed something fundamental and unchangeable in his nature. Hassan found it as hard to understand the way she thought as she did to understand the way he did.

Gravely he said, 'I mentioned that Mr Findlay had asked to be shown around the house, and had asked me many questions, particularly about the master's art collection.'

Keira's stomach sank. That's it, then, she thought. Hassan has warned Ivo before I got a chance, and now Ivo is going to believe I was conspiring behind his back, that I deliberately brought Gerard here.

'The master was displeased,' Hassan added simply, his fixed gaze on her face.

'I'll talk to him,' she said again. 'I'll ring him immediately.'

Hassan bowed and moved out of the way. Keira walked past him into the house, feeling his reproachful stare on her all the way.

It was at that instant that she knew she was going to have to leave the villa, and go at once. She could not stay here another day. She would book a fight for tomorrow.

She rang Florida immediately; her mother answered the phone, and began to giggle, firing off questions at her. If there was one subject Elise adored it was that of the opposite sex. She loved to gossip about men, about affairs, who was seeing whom, what marriage was on the rocks, who was having a secret fling. 'Darling,' she cooed, 'so you're dating that drop-dead gorgeous TV reporter! Why have you kept it quiet? How long has it been going on? Is it serious? Is he married?'

'We're just good friends,' Keira said lightly, and heard her mother gurgling with amusement.

'Not that old chestnut! Oh, come on, darling! He doesn't look the platonic type to me. All man,

I'd say. I saw him stripped on TV once—swimming across some river somewhere, with a lot of soldiers carrying rifles over their heads. He had taken off his shirt and we saw lots of lovely smooth tanned skin, all rippling with muscle. I fancied him myself.'

Keira's teeth met. She almost reminded her mother that she was a good fifteen years older than Gerard, but Elise would never have forgiven her for it, so she bit back the words.

'I thought Sara was joining you,' Elise said slyly. 'You told us wicked fibs, darling. You're very secretive. Ivo is furious. He says you've shocked Hassan. You were silly, darling; you should never have brought Gerard Findlay back to the villa. If you had met him in Tangier at his hotel Hassan would never have known, and you'd have saved yourself a lot of trouble.'

Furious, Keira said, 'Is Ivo there? I rang to talk to him.'

'He left,' her mother said. 'Two hours ago. He's going somewhere or other on business.'

'Oh,' Keira said, taken aback. 'When will he be back? Did he say?'

'No, he never tells me anything, you know that.'

'Well, when he does get back will you tell him to ring me here? I'm leaving tomorrow...'

'So soon? But isn't Sara joining you at all? What is going on, darling? You haven't quarrelled with that gorgeous man already, have you? You're always so stupid about men, Keira. You simply don't know how to handle them. You have to humour then, let them have their own way; it makes them easier to handle when you want something really badly. If you want to keep a man you have to be clever, darling.'

Through her teeth Keira said, 'Sorry, I have to go now, Elise. Bye.' She hung up without waiting for her mother to reply, then she rang the airport and managed to book herself on to the first flight in the morning. After that she rang Sara to explain that she wasn't staying in Tangier; she was coming home next day.

Sara was almost tearful. 'Oh, Keira, I ruined your holiday, didn't I?'

'Don't be silly!'

'If I hadn't cried off you wouldn't be coming back so soon!'

'It has nothing to do with you. I've run into problems here. I can't talk about it on the phone; I'll explain when I see you. I shall be back tomorrow afternoon; I'll ring you then.'

She waited all evening for Ivo to ring, but no phone call came and in a state of nervous tension she went to bed early that evening, having informed Hassan and Alima that she was leaving next day. Hassan was unperturbed, Alima clearly upset, but, with her brother around, she said very little. It was obvious to Keira that Hassan had told Alima the truth about Gerard, and the fact that Keira had, in effect, lied to them, and also, no doubt, added the news that Ivo Krensky had been very angry when Hassan told him how Gerard had visited the villa and asked so many questions.

Keira didn't sleep well; she tossed and turned all night, worrying about her mother, and Ivo, and the threat of the police arriving at the villa. When she finally fell into restless sleep she had bad dreams, confused and disturbing dreams in which she ran from a faceless man through a darkened house which was sometimes the villa in Tangier and sometimes her own home back in Chelsea. Twisting and turning, she fled through empty rooms and then through crowds which inexplicably appeared and vanished; but the figure behind her kept coming; she could not escape it. At last she turned to face her pursuer; he was masked; she saw the glitter of eyes through narrow slits. He put a hand up to his face to remove his mask and she screamed in utter terror...

Waking up with a jolt, she found herself sitting upright in bed, trembling violently. There had been no face under the mask, just emptiness. She had felt herself falling into it, down into utter darkness.

A second later there was the sound of running feet, then agitated tapping on her door.

'Miss Keira? Is something wrong?'

Breathlessly she called out, 'Sorry, Alima, I had a nightmare. I'm OK, though—sorry if I woke you.'

Her voice concerned, Alima asked, 'Can I get you anything? A drink?'

'No, thanks; go back to bed, Alima.'

'I was just going to get up anyway,' Alima told her, and Keira switched on the light to look at the clock and was surprised to see that it was nearly six.

'I shall have to get up soon myself,' she said with a weary yawn. 'I have to pack before Hassan drives me to the airport.'

'Let me pack for you,' Alima offered. 'I will get your breakfast and bring it up, then while you eat I will pack for you.'

'You're very kind, Alima. Thank you.'

Keira slid out of bed and went to the window, opened the shutters and saw the rosy morning glow on the horizon which meant that the sun was rising. The birds had begun to call in the flame trees and magnolias; the air was fresh and cool.

She padded barefoot into the bathroom and had a shower, blow-dried her red hair, then dressed in comfortable green cotton trousers and a pale lime shirt.

Alima arrived with her breakfast while she was getting the rest of her clothes out of the wardrobe, ready to pack them.

'Let me deal with that,' she said, placing the tray of food on the table on the balcony.

'There's no need; I can manage!' protested Keira.

'I would like to do that for you,' said Alima very seriously, and Keira smiled at her gratefully before going out on to the balcony to eat.

She wasn't hungry, but Alima had only brought her croissants, rolls and cherry jam, juice, coffee and a bowl of fruit.

Keira sipped orange juice and then drank some coffee with a croissant. While she was eating she heard the sound of a car coming through the gates, crunching over the gravel of the drive, and her stomach turned over. She jumped to her feet in alarm, pale with nerves.

It couldn't be Gerard at this hour! Unless... What if he had rung the police? What if the arrivals were policemen with a warrant to search the villa?

'Who can that be?' Alima asked from inside her room, having also heard the arrival.

Keira went back inside and found her bedroom door open and Alima standing in the corridor, listening intently to the sounds below on the ground floor. Hassan's voice floated up to them, and then Keira heard a very familiar brusque, coarse voice.

Ivo! she thought in shock.

Alima turned to stare at her, open-mouthed, her face reflecting Keira's incredulity.

'The master!'

'Yes.'

'But . . . he was in Florida . . .'

'He must have flown through the night,' Keira said, suddenly very cold and shaky. The call from Hassan must have put the fear of God into Ivo. Was her mother with him? Or had he come alone? Did her mother even know he had come to Tangier? Maybe he had left before she rang Elise yesterday afternoon? After all, Elise had said she had no idea where he was or when he would be back. Keira could remember many times when Ivo had simply gone away without explaining why or where he was going. She had put it down to his love of mystery, his dislike of explaining himself and what he was doing—but now she wondered if his disappearances had always had a more sinister explanation.

What exactly was Ivo mixed up in?

A moment later they both heard the soft tread of sandalled feet on the stairs and Hassan appeared at the end of the corridor. Alima began to greet him but he held up his hand, rapidly said something in Arabic, which made her fall silent, her face anxious.

Turning to Keira, Hassan said gravely, 'The master wishes to see you at once, miss, in his suite.'

Keira nodded, taking a deep breath. She wasn't looking forward to facing Ivo, but there was no way out. She had to go through with it.

The normally locked door of the private suite stood open; she paused to look in and saw Ivo standing by the window, his heavy body outlined in the golden glow of the morning.

He glared at her across the room, a large, balding man with thick features and hard eyes. 'Come in and shut the door.'

His harsh voice grated on her nerves. It always had. She had been wary of him from the minute they'd met, although she had only been a child then. Grief and love made you hypersensitive, especially when you were very young and other impressions had not dulled your reactions.

She had never liked him, but now she was actually scared of him. There was something dangerous in his face, the glare of a wild animal which had been frightened and was angry, might even kill, if that was what it took to protect itself, she thought, her heart in her mouth.

'Is my mother with you——?' she began, but he cut her off.

'No, and don't bring her into this. I've just had to fly from Florida all night and I'm in no mood for small talk.'

'Have you asked Hassan to get you breakfast? I——'

'Shut up!' he snarled. 'I came here to find out what the hell you've been up to. How dare you bring a reporter into my home and let him quiz my servants? And don't tell me he was just chatting to Hassan, or try to convince me that he's simply your boyfriend. I rang a few people and I found out that Findlay has a reputation as a tough nut. I also found out that his company is poking about making a nuisance of itself, and you can tell him from me that he'll get himself into serious trouble if he pries into my affairs. What happened to him during that civil war could happen again—only this time he won't get over it!'

Flushing in anger, Keira snapped at him, 'Are you mad? You can't make threats like that and get away with it.'

He glared at her. 'I'm not threatening anything. If I tell you that if you go out into the rain without an umbrella you'll get wet, that isn't a threat, it's just a statement of fact. And if Findlay pokes his nose where it isn't wanted someone will cut off his whole damn head!'

'I'll tell him you said so,' Keira said furiously. 'I'm sure he'll use that quote on the programme.'

Ivo stood very still. 'So, there's going to be a programme, is there? I guessed, from what Hassan told me. It was obvious Findlay was after something—did he tell you what it was?'

'You,' Keira said tersely.

He was shocked into silence for a second. He had probably been hoping that Gerard was just being nosy and didn't know actually anything.

'He's working on an investigation into an art racket,' Keira flatly expanded.

She heard his thick intake of breath but he didn't speak, so she went on.

'He says there's a ring of art thieves operating on an international scale. They steal to order—rich collectors want certain paintings, can't buy them on the open market because they're public property and never come on the market, so they commission professional art thieves to get hold of them.'

She heard Ivo swear brutally under his breath, then he pulled himself up, saying offhandedly, 'And has he got any proof? Or is he just dreaming up fairy-stories?'

'It isn't a fairy-story, Ivo, is it?'

'How would I know?'

She gave him a cold, ironic stare. 'Don't play the innocent with me, Ivo. He came to Tangier in search of proof, I suspect—because he believes you're involved.'

'He told you that?' Ivo asked sharply.

'Yes.'

His voice thickened. 'And you let him into my house and let him poke and pry about, question Hassan, get——'

'He wanted to see your private collection.'

The air between them quivered with rage. Ivo visibly fought for control, forced a short laugh. 'Private collection? What are you talking about?'

She was tired of fencing with him. 'Stop playing games, Ivo! You know very well what I mean. The paintings in your private suite.'

His voice hoarse, Ivo said, 'What have you been feeding him?'

'He asked if you had any other paintings and I told him you had some in your own private rooms— I'd no idea that it was a big secret, or why you wanted it kept locked.'

'I keep it locked to make sure it's safe!' he blustered. 'I don't want to be burgled. And you can tell your reporter friend that that suite is electronically monitored night and day—not a mouse could stir in it without setting off alarms both in the villa and in the police station. If he tries to break in he'll find himself in a Moroccan gaol, and he could be there for a long, long time.'

'He wouldn't try to burgle that suite! He isn't stupid.' She took a deep breath. 'I'm afraid he knows about that Australian painting; he saw a——'

'What did you say?' Ivo broke in hoarsely.

'The Australian desert painting...'

'I know which one you mean!' Ivo shouted. 'Why the hell did you tell him about it? What else have you told him?'

'I didn't tell him—he saw a photo of it in my house in the mews.'

'What? How did you get hold of a photo of it?'

Her face whitening at the snarl of his voice, she snapped back at him, 'My mother sent me some photos taken in your suite during that party you gave the last time I stayed at the villa. Some of your paintings could be seen in them. Gerard recognised one of the paintings as having been stolen from a public gallery.'

'My God, the stupid bitch!' Ivo breathed. 'She never told me she'd taken any photos, let alone sent them to you!'

'Don't talk about her like that! She didn't take the pictures; she can't have because she's in them— I think some friend of yours did, and sent her copies.'

'And she sent them to you! I had no idea any photos existed. If I'd known I'd have——' He broke off, but she could guess the rest of the sentence.

He would have destroyed the photos if he had known about them.

Keira looked at him with loathing. 'Did my mother know what was going on? Did she know those paintings were stolen property?'

'Who says they are? Your boyfriend? He's crazy.'

'Don't lie to me! All I want to know is . . . is my mother involved?'

There was silence. His heavy black brows met and he looked away, his mouth working. Then he muttered, 'No. You don't think I'm so crazy I'd tell her anything? She's too damn stupid. Oh, not that she'd disapprove, but she'd tell someone; she can't keep secrets. She'd think it was all some sort of game.'

Deeply relieved, Keira closed her eyes, then opened them again. 'Why, Ivo? Why did you do it? You have plenty of money, you can buy anything you want—why risk going to prison just for a painting?'

'Why do you go on eating jags and then throw up?' he asked crudely.

She swallowed on a wave of nausea. Yes. Why do I? she thought with bitterness and pain. Why am I such a psychological mess? Who did it to me? Myself? Or other people?

Ivo met her eyes and suddenly grimaced. 'I never liked you, you know. You were a sullen, awkward little brat and I knew you resented me from the start—and it was mutual. A pity your father wouldn't have you; we offered you to him but he didn't want to know.'

Pain jabbed inside her. He wasn't telling her anything new, but it still hurt.

'You were in our way. Elise and me, we didn't need a brat hanging around, but we were stuck with you. And don't look at me as if I'd gutted you. You may not know why you have an eating problem but I can work it out. I'm not apologising; I learnt survival in a tough school and it was you or me, kid. I needed Elise more than you did. OK, you had a tough time when you were a kid—but I had it tougher, believe me. I've been to hell and back, and that's why I need to have paintings.'

He saw her scornful expression and glared, his thick neck red with temper, eyes bulging. 'Yes, I used the word need. And it fits. Collecting gets to be an obsession, I guess. It isn't just a whim, for God's sake. I can't help myself.'

She stared at him, wondering what sort of creature he really was, this crude, ferocious animal of a man, with his drive and his bad tempers, his possessive instincts. He had deliberately cut her off from her mother whenever he could; it wasn't enough for him to have married Elise—he needed to own her, exclusively.

Ivo turned away and stood at the window, staring out. After a moment he began to mutter over his shoulder, 'You don't know anything about me, girl. You know nothing about what makes me tick. When the Press write about me they call me a self-made man, and that's the exact truth. I am self-made. The man you know, the man the world sees, is self-made. There was another Ivo Krensky once, long ago.'

She was puzzled, frowning. Another one? What did he mean?

His voice slowed to a reluctant murmur. 'I was born in Odessa. In 1929. Even telling you that isn't telling you anything you understand, because you know nothing about the world I come from.'

He walked away from the window and took down a large, framed poster, in the modernistic primary colours and shapes of the art deco period popular during the 1920s.

'Have you ever looked at this?'

She had never even seen it before. It was a poster for a film, a flight of stone steps, soldiers with fixed bayonets, dull grey and blue with a splash of terrifying red where a dead man lay in a pool of blood.

'Eisenstein.' She read the director's name printed in black lettering down one side of the poster, recognising it, and remembering having once seen the film. '*Potemkin.*'

Ivo nodded. '*The Battleship Potemkin*, a great Russian film. It was a real incident, in Odessa, in 1905, a mutiny by sailors on the battleship, a workers' strike at the same time—the government sent out the army.'

She shivered involuntarily. 'I remember the famous scene, on the steps...a pram bumping down the steps with a baby crying in it.'

'That's the film. Odessa is a beautiful city; in spring there are chestnut trees in flower in the streets, we have beaches and wide avenues, and these steps...the Potemkin staircase they call it now...they're magnificent...built of granite. After the Revolution the men who died there became heroes, had statues put up to them. Where I lived was ugly, though. Modern concrete canyons of grey blocks of flats. Depressing just to live there. We had nothing. We lived in one room almost at the top of the building with a view of nothing but roofs.'

'When did you leave Russia?' she ventured warily.

'I'm not Russian,' he snarled, exploding into rage again. 'I'm Ukrainian.' His eyes spat contempt. 'You don't even know that! Odessa is in the Ukraine. The Russians captured it during a war with the Turks, under Catherine the Great, and they never left. We've been a slave race for centuries.'

Startled, she said, 'But I'd always assumed...everyone did, and you never said you weren't Russian!'

'I learnt very young to hold my tongue,' he said curtly. 'A pity you didn't.'

She bit back the angry retort; she didn't want him clamming up again.

He hung the framed poster up on the wall again, muttering over his shoulder at her. 'This was the first picture I ever managed to get. I stole it from an exhibition of poster art in New York in the late forties. That was what started me off collecting. I had always had the taste for art, never had the money for years.'

'So you stole?' she asked scathingly and he turned on her.

'Don't go all pious on me, missy! When I saw that poster I had to have it, to remind me... The one good thing about life in the Soviet Union in those days was the museums and galleries; they were free and they were full of the most dazzling, lovely things.'

His voice was full of feeling; she listened intently, feeling a fugitive sympathy for the man, although she had always disliked him intensely until now.

'When you're hungry you dream of food,' he said, eyes glittering. 'My father was a sailor, my mother worked gutting fish in the fish market. I always had enough to eat, a sort of porridge for breakfast, or black bread, fish soup for the midday meal and fish for supper with more black bread— it was rough food but it was filling. But I hated the way we lived; it was harsh and brutish. If it hadn't been for my grandfather... He was an artist.'

Ah! she thought. So that was where it came from. It had to have come from somewhere, this obsession of his.

'He was never very good,' Ivo said, his mouth twisting wryly. 'But he was passionate about art. He ended up as a scene painter at the Opera House in Odessa, earning a pittance. It wasn't full-time work; he only worked when they needed new backcloths. As my parents were both at work, he stayed in our cramped little flat with me, told me about European art, showed me pictures in books, took me to the museum, to art galleries, taught me to draw and paint. He took me backstage at the opera, to see the work he did. I longed to be a painter when I grew up, but I didn't have the talent, either. It's our family curse—the love of painting, without the talent.'

She felt that jab of sympathy for him again. It must be painful to feel the urge to create without having the ability to do so.

'Is your grandfather still alive?'

Furiously he snapped, 'Don't be stupid! If he was, he'd be over a hundred. He was an old man when I was born. He died when I was eight, but he left a deep impression on me.'

He didn't need to tell her that; it was obvious. For the first time she had heard real emotion in his voice, and his face had been lit with it, with an angry, almost despairing sort of love.

Ivo walked to the window again and stood with his back to her, staring out. 'When I realised I would never be able to paint either, I decided I'd still have paintings around me; I'd buy them, when I had money, and when I did nobody else would ever be allowed to see them. I'd be the only one who could look at them. Oh, it was just a stupid childish daydream; I'd no chance of being rich, not while I lived in Odessa.'

'You've never told me how you got out.'

'Habit,' he grunted. 'It was safer not to talk about it for a long time and then I just didn't want to. I got out when I was nine. War was coming, we all knew it, and 1938 was a bad year for us. My mother died, having another baby, and in the winter my grandfather died of pneumonia. My father was a Ukrainian nationalist, a dangerous thing to be during the Stalin years; someone informed on him and we had to go into hiding. We hid in the cata-combs for months.'

'Catacombs?' she repeated, startled.

'They're caves which run for hundreds of miles underground—for centuries they've been used by criminals, outcasts, down-and-outs. They're cold and damp and there's no light down there, but the police couldn't find you once you got in there.

There were too many passages. We couldn't stay there forever, though. My father had a friend—a Turk, the captain of a freighter which sailed between Odessa and Istanbul. The Turk once got into a fight with some Russian sailors on the quayside; he was knocked out and thrown into the harbour and would have drowned, but my father dived in and rescued him. The Turk felt he owed my father a life. He smuggled us both out on his freighter.'

'That must have been very dangerous!' Keira had never suspected his life story would be as dramatic as this; her eyes were enormous as she listened.

He laughed angrily. 'Of course it was. If we'd been found when the ship was searched before it left port, we would all have been arrested, put on trial, then shot.'

She believed him; her face paled. 'How did he hide you during the search?'

'He was carrying mainly timber but he had some crates of vodka in the hold. One of the crates had a false bottom. The vodka was on top. We were under a board below that.'

'Were you frightened?' He had been nine years old, she thought; it must have been a terrifying experience for such a young child.

His voice was contemptuous. 'What do you think? I was nine years old, and very small for my age, we were cramped into one position, we couldn't move an inch, it was pitch-black and airless, the ship went through pretty rough weather, we were tossed about, and were both very seasick, which didn't make life any more comfortable. Fortunately, we hadn't eaten for two days before that, or it would have been much worse. We had to stay inside the crate without food or drink for three more days until we reached Turkey and then we had to be smuggled off the ship again. The Turkish authorities would have sent us back if they had found us.'

'How did you get to America from Turkey?' He must have been tough to have survived that voyage, she thought, appalled by all he had told her.

He shrugged. 'My father's friend lent us the money; I don't suppose he ever expected to get it back but we did repay the loan within five years. My father got a job working in the docks in New York and I went to school. I got a job as soon as I could, and I began making money. That was when I discovered that although I couldn't paint I had a talent—I could sell. I worked in street markets, then I got a job as a salesman with a tractor company, in the mid-west; I travelled right across the States and then I met a man on the road who was trying to sell plastic buckets, and I realised the potential market in plastic. I set up my own company and it took off like a train.'

'So that's how you made all your money? In plastic?'

'First plastic, then electronics,' he shrugged. 'Computers, mainly. Then I bought into the video market...I have a lucky touch where money is concerned. I can't seem to help making it.' His dark eyes glared at her. 'And it was all legitimate. I made my money honestly. As soon as I could afford it, I started buying paintings. I used to reward myself for having pulled off a big deal.' His voice thickened. 'I'd buy the best painting I could afford. Slowly I began to put together a collection. Now I have some marvellous things, but I can never have enough.' She heard the deep vibration in his throat, the hoarseness of hunger. 'There aren't enough paintings in the world to keep me satisfied; I have to keep buying more and more, and sometimes I get obsessed with one I can't have——'

He broke off and Keira flatly finished the sentence for him.

'And you arrange for it to be stolen?'

'I didn't say that! Don't put words in my mouth!' His rage had returned; his voice was furry with hatred. 'And don't sit in judgement on me either! I told you all that so that you would understand why I have to have these...'

He gestured around the room, at the walls, crowded with paintings.

'But you still don't understand, do you?' His face convulsed. 'And you never will. You and your mother...you're both stupid bitches. You betrayed me to this reporter; I never want to set eyes on you again, do you hear? Pack your bags and get out of my house.'

'I'm going,' she said. 'I fly this morning. But I have one thing to say to you—I don't care if I never see you again, but don't try to stop me seeing my mother because if you do I'll tell her what you've got yourself involved in, and I can see you don't want her to know.'

His jawline clenched; he didn't answer.

'I mean it,' Keira said.

'If she wants to see you, I won't stop her,' Ivo ground out through his teeth.

She nodded. 'Then I'd be grateful if Hassan could drive me to the airport.'

'He can't. Take a taxi. I'll need Hassan here.' Ivo walked away and began taking pictures down from the walls.

He was going to have them all moved out of the house, she realised, hesitating. Where to? But what was that to her? She would never see Ivo again, probably.

She went out and walked downstairs. The phone was ringing; Hassan answered it, said with icy courtesy, 'No, sir, she is not available. I am sorry.'

He put the phone down and turned to look at Keira in a way that made her nerves prickle.

'Was that for me?' she asked, beginning to be angry.

The dark eyes were polite but steady. 'I am sorry; my master has ordered me not to allow you to talk on the telephone to Mr Findlay.'

'That was him?' But she had already guessed it from something in Hassan's very eloquent body language. He had a capacity for conveying what he thought and felt without saying a word.

Hassan nodded, watching her impassively.

'How do you know I haven't already rung him?' she threw at him.

'Please excuse me, but I have monitored your calls.'

She drew breath, outraged. 'And if I had rung him?'

'I would have cut you off.'

Keira stared at Hassan's graceful, still figure in the dark djellabah, the calm, reproachful eyes. He did not understand her. She did not understand him. But she liked him and she regretted the gulf

between them. I can't wait to get home, she
thought. I can't wait to leave all this behind me.

'Would you ring for a taxi for me, please?'

'I have done so, miss,' Hassan informed her. 'It
is coming.'

It arrived five minutes later and she drove off in
it without looking back. As the taxi approached
the villa gates a large van drove through them,
heading for the house. Was it coming to remove
the stolen pictures? If Gerard didn't arrive with the
police soon he would be too late; there would be
no evidence against Ivo.

He'll blame me, thought Keira, staring out at the
blue sky which glittered with hot sunlight. He'll
know I warned Ivo. He's going to be furious. What
will he do?

He can't eat you, she reassured herself.

No, but he can chew me up and spit out the
pieces!

She didn't look forward to facing him in a really
bad temper, especially as he had every reason to be
angry with her.

You won't have to! said that cynical inner voice
which spoke from her very depths, charged with all
the pain and rejection she had suffered in the past.
Gerard will probably never speak to you again.

Her body winced in intolerable grief. She knew
him so well now. She knew that was the most likely
outcome.

How was she going to bear living next door to
him knowing he hated her? He had managed to
ignore her and Sara for months after he'd first
moved in; he would do so again. She was in no

doubt about his ability to be ruthless, merciless with anyone he felt had failed him.

She would have to see him go in and out day after day, so close and yet as unreachable as if he lived on another planet.

CHAPTER EIGHT

KEIRA got back to Chelsea late in the afternoon. The weather was hot, sultry, a lurid light flashing across London's skyline, the streets airless. A storm was coming.

She felt intensely lonely as she closed her front door. The place was empty, silent; so was the little mews cottage next door. Gerard would still be in Tangier. Maybe he would never come back here. Ivo would no doubt try to get him out; Gerard probably had a year's lease, if not more, but sooner or later Ivo was going to make him pay for having started that investigation. Gerard would go. Would that be worse than having him around but ignoring her?

Keira didn't know; all she did know was that she felt as if she had fallen off the world and was free-falling through space. She was out of control again, her head throbbing, her body shaking. She hadn't been able to cry while she was travelling. She hadn't eaten, either, although her stomach had clamoured for food; she had craved it all the time. She had averted her eyes from the other people around her when they'd eaten on the plane. She hadn't allowed herself to eat because she was afraid that once she started she wouldn't be able to stop and people would start to stare.

Now that she was alone she began to run to the kitchen, tears raining down her face. She began the frantic hunt for food, trembling, sobbing: crisps, biscuits, cake, tins of baked beans, tins of oranges, pineapples, a large piece of cheddar cheese, sliced ham in vacuum packets. It had to be instant; she couldn't wait to cook anything; she just needed the fix of it in her mouth. It was all flung out on the table while she took bites out of everything, eating so fast she didn't taste it, crying all the time while she crammed food into her mouth.

The phone began to ring. She ignored it. It rang and rang, then stopped. Keira began drinking milk from the fridge, gulping it down. The phone began again. She ignored it. It stopped. A moment later it began again, and it was beginning to get on her nerves.

'Shut up!' she screamed at it, but it went on and on and on until she could stand it no longer and snatched it up, yelling, 'Will you stop ringing?' into it.

'Keira?'

It was Sara, sounding alarmed at once.

'Please, just leave me alone,' Keira groaned, and hung up.

But the call had broken the circle; she looked at the food scattered all over the kitchen and felt her stomach heave. Oh, God, she thought, I've done it again.

Running for the stairs, she stumbled up them, sobbing, into the bathroom, despising herself. A few minutes later she ran lukewarm water into the bath; while she waited she splashed cold water on to her feverish, tear-stained face and cleaned her teeth obsessively for minutes at a time, feeling unclean, as she always did after an eating jag.

When was she was going to break out of the circle for good? she thought despairingly. She had thought she had; but this was the second time she had lost control in just a couple of weeks.

Naked, she climbed into the comforting rose-perfumed water of the bath, leaned back, eyes closed, trembling violently. Thank heavens Sara had rung, or she might have gone on eating for hours. Once she lost control it was so hard to get herself back on track.

But you did, she thought. You stopped. Once even Sara's call wouldn't have stopped you; nothing would. You wouldn't have answered the phone; it could have rung for hours and you'd have ignored it. Stop running yourself down. Don't tell yourself you're a hopeless case; that's the same as giving yourself permission to slide backwards, give up, stop fighting. And that's the worse thing you could do.

Downstairs she heard the phone ringing again. She would ring Sara back later, reassure her that she wasn't in desperate need of help, she needn't panic. Sara was vulnerable herself at the moment; she ought to be resting, taking care of herself. Keira didn't want Sara feeling she had to drag herself all the way up to London from her home in the country just to check that she was OK.

Then her mouth quivered into a smile; at least Sara cared about her. That made her feel less like somebody in an empty landscape.

At that instant the bathroom was lit by a flash of lightning that made her start, eyes flying open. The storm had arrived; she heard a roll of thunder somewhere in the city.

The sky was as black as midnight out there; so was the bathroom; she hadn't put on the light and now she could hardly see a hand in front of her face. Keira shivered, afraid of the dark, climbed hurriedly out of the bath, dripping, and put on a towelling robe, dried her feet and legs, pulled the plug out of the bath and while the water was gurgling down the drain walked into her bedroom.

She lay down on top of her bed, shivering every time the lightning flashed and the thunder roared. The storm seemed to have got inside her head; she was the sky in which the elements raged. Round and round in circles her thoughts went and got nowhere; she tried to understand Ivo, Gerard, Hassan, all those men, so complicated and so hard to fathom. Their motives and feelings were too alien to her very female instincts. She just kept thinking, Why? Why?

But how could she fathom them when she couldn't work herself out?

Exhaustion, mental and physical, caught up with her after a while and she slid into a light doze, only to wake up abruptly at a sound, just heard through the continuing crash of the storm outside.

Her eyes opened and Keira sat up, felt her heart soar into her mouth as the door of her bedroom slowly opened.

A scream choked in her throat. A dark shape filled the doorway, seemed to fill the room, towering over her, a faceless threat. The silence was crowded with shadows and fears.

Then a deep, angry voice said, 'You stupid woman! What have you done to yourself?' and the light came on, blinding her.

She looked at him incredulously, green eyes glazed, slitted like a cat's against the vicious glare of electricity. He was wearing an open-necked white shirt, no tie, grey trousers, a lightweight pale grey jacket which showed dark spots of rain.

She almost felt she was having hallucinations; light-headed with exhaustion and emotional turmoil, she had conjured him up from her sub-conscious. He couldn't be here.

'You're in Tangier,' she stupidly said.

'I flew back on the plane after yours and came straight here. I wasn't sure what sort of state you would be in.'

She looked away from his watchful eyes, furious because he had obviously seen the state the kitchen was in and knew that she had lost control again. It had only happened twice in the past year—why had he been around each time?

'You've been sick?' he asked, and she hated him for being right.

She shouted back at him, 'Will you stop breaking into my house? I'm beginning to think you're really a professional burglar, not a reporter. I'll get someone to come round and fit bolts on the front door—you won't be able to break in so easily then!'

'I shall be moving out soon anyway.'

The cool announcement knocked all the breath out of her. She sat there, staring, the words rever-berating inside her head. He was going, moving out, leaving the mews. She would never see him again. It hurt so much that she couldn't even react. She was paralysed with pain.

Gerard watched her pale, stiff face as though trying to read whatever lay behind the mask. His mouth twisted, his eyes flashed.

'Well, that really upset you, didn't it?' He ran a hand through his black hair, raking it back angrily.

'What did you want me to do? Burst into tears?' she muttered, then wished she hadn't said it aloud because she was on the point of doing just that. She swallowed down the saltiness of her pain and hurriedly changed the subject to something more down-to-earth and less emotion-charged.

'I . . . I thought you had a year's lease on the cottage?'

'I do, but your stepfather tells me he won't be renewing it when it ends. I've decided to buy myself a flat in a new block nearer the TV studios.'

'You saw him in Tangier?' She was dismayed to hear it. What had Ivo said to him? She was relieved she hadn't been there.

'Early this morning, just after you'd left for the airport, I gather.' His tone was ironic, his face as polished and dangerous as a dagger. 'He insisted on showing me his private suite.'

'Had he . . . were the . . . pictures still . . .?'

Gerard laughed curtly. 'What do you think? As I drove towards the house I saw a van driving away. I suspect it was loaded with the pictures.'

So Ivo had got the pictures away! She made an involuntary move and the folds of her robe fell apart. Gerard looked down at that brief glimpse of her bare thighs, the rough curls of red-gold hair between them.

Appalled and very flushed, she hurriedly pulled the robe together again, covering herself up. Good

God! He might think she'd done that deliberately. If you believed the psychologists every lapse like that was secretly deliberate; the conscious mind simply preferred to call it an accident when it was no such thing.

'Had you got the police with you?' she quickly asked.

His eyes lifted with visible reluctance. 'No. But then I didn't realise your stepfather was back in Tangier, did I?' Accusation showed in his face for a moment. 'You wouldn't talk to me when I rang you last night and again early this morning. All I got was friend Hassan being politely icy, telling me you couldn't come to the phone. I had set the wheels in motion, told my colleague in London that I was pretty sure there were stolen pictures in the house— he wanted to get a camera team out to Tangier to film, and he immediately got in touch with Interpol's art squad, but the wheels of the police grind almost as slowly as the wheels of God and it takes an age to get together a camera team as well.'

'So you went to the villa on your own?'

'To see you,' he said. 'To try to talk you out of warning your stepfather. But I was too late, wasn't I?' His grey eyes were hard and angry. 'You had told him, and he had had time to get the pictures away.'

'I didn't have to tell him,' she said flatly. 'Hassan did, on the phone, while I was at your hotel.'

His brows met. 'Hassan? He was in on the racket?'

She frowned too because she didn't want to believe that; she liked Hassan and respected him. 'I doubt it. I think Hassan is honest. No, he just told

Ivo about you—who you were, what your name was, that you had visited me, asked to be shown around the house and asked some very searching questions about your art collection. Maybe Hassan thought you were planning to burgle the place? But Ivo knew who you were, and he had a guilty conscience—he didn't want you taking a close interest in his art collection for fear of what you might find out.'

'So he flew to Tangier,' Gerard said tersely.

'Overnight.' The back of her neck ached; so did her head. The strain was getting to her again. Did he have to look at her as if he hated her? 'What will happen now?' she asked him. 'Will your friend's investigation go on? Will he bring Ivo into the programme?'

'Without the evidence of the paintings? Not unless the company wants to be sued for slander.' His narrowed eyes focused on her. 'Would you go on the programme and tell everything you know about your stepfather's collection?'

She hesitated, then shook her head. 'Even if I did, I'm no expert; I can't tell a copy from an original.'

He didn't seem surprised. 'Did you know last night that he was coming?' he asked through his teeth.

'No! It was a big shock to me when he arrived. He started moving the pictures out right away.' Her voice was brittle, but she pretended to smile gaily. 'He moved me out too. And I won't be invited back. He thinks I betrayed him, plotted with you against him. He never wants to see me again, he told me—not that he ever wanted to see me in the first place.'

She laughed raggedly. 'Well, at least it's out in the open, and official. My stepfather hates me. He told me he always had.'

Gerard watched her, frowning darkly. Her eyes were too bright and there was a feverish circle of red in each cheek.

'He didn't need to tell me that. I always knew, right from the start, that he didn't want me around.'

Gerard swore under his breath. 'The man's a bastard.'

'I won't argue,' she said lightly.

'What about your mother? Will he let you see her?'

She gave him a fixed, unreal smile. 'He said if she wants to that's her business. But knowing my mother she won't bother often. She never has before—why would she start now? She's a busy woman, she has a crowded social life, and she was never the maternal type.'

'I had a feeling something like that had happened,' Gerard muttered. 'That's why I came here straight from the airport instead of going into the office, as I ought to have done, to talk to the programme team about what happened in Tangier. I knew something was wrong with you.'

Her heart missed a beat. Was he saying he cared? That it mattered to him?

'I was terrified,' Gerard said harshly, his eyes dark. 'I was afraid you might——' He broke off, his throat moving convulsively as he swallowed. 'And I was right, wasn't I? I've seen the kitchen—you've done it again. You've had another eating jag.'

Trembling and feverish, she whispered, 'I stopped. I started to binge, but I stopped myself!' She tried to laugh it off, shrugged and said lightly, 'And I don't need any lectures on how stupid it is; I know all about that—and you aren't my analyst!'

'But my God, you need one!' he snarled, and was suddenly on her side of the room, inches away from her.

She started violently, her colour coming and going, her eyes dilated with fear and desire.

'Don't you lay a finger on me, mister, or I'll hit you with something!'

She was intensely aware that she was only wearing a towelling robe under which she was completely naked. A hot blush swept up her face; she dragged the lapels of the robe together and held them with both hands while she swung her legs off the bed. He watched her every move.

His voice turned husky, softer. 'You don't need to be frightened of me, Keira,' he said, and her chin went up in defiance and rebellion. She couldn't take much more pain from him, or from life itself, at that moment. She was just about coping; she knew it wouldn't take much to push her over the edge and next time she might not be able to get herself together again. Like Humpty-Dumpty she would be in pieces and not all the king's men, not whole regiments of them, would put her back together.

'You don't scare me!' she threw at him.

'Well, you sure as hell scare me,' Gerard said, making her catch her breath. He looked down at her. 'I've been fighting the way I feel about you ever since I saw you for the first time. I wanted to get you into bed there and then.'

Her heart turned over sickeningly. But her mind fiercely resisted, telling her, Don't listen; don't let him reach you.

'But I'd only just broken up with my previous girlfriend,' he said with an angry twist of the mouth. 'I was in no mood to get involved with anyone else. I wouldn't let myself want you. As long as I stayed out of your way I had no problem, but when Sara came banging on my door that day because she was worried about you I couldn't help getting involved and before I knew where I was it was too late. You'd got me.'

She was both furious and excited. What did he mean, she had 'got' him? As though she had set a trap and caught him! Was that what he thought?

'Well, I don't want you.' But her voice was breathless, betraying her, and his eyes glittered.

'We both know you do, just as we both know I want you,' he said, reaching for her.

She was thrown into panic at once, shaking her head, but when she tried to move away her knees hit the edge of the bed and she stumbled off balance.

Gerard stopped her from falling, his hands closing on her shoulders, steadying her, then he abruptly pulled her, struggling, towards him. She tried to thrust him off, her hands splayed against his chest.

It was a mistake to touch him. She knew that a second later as the heat of his body under the thin silky shirt percolated through her palms, crept under her skin and up through her veins.

Oh, God, I can't stand much more of this! she thought, dying to push his shirt aside and touch him. She would willingly spend the rest of eternity touching him, slowly, intimately, with passion.

Don't even think about it! she told herself, mouth dry. It will only end in you getting hurt. Love always does.

He bent his head and she turned hers away, fighting him. His mouth hunted over her face, kissed her ear, her neck, her cheek, her jawline, moving inexorably to her mouth.

As soon as he reached it Keira was lost. She heard the groan of satisfaction he gave as he finally took her mouth, and made the same hoarse sounds herself; her lips parted, her body turned weak and plastic, swayed towards him in helpless attraction as the hunger took over. Perspiration sprang out on her skin; her arms went round him.

Gerard pushed her down on to the bed again, without taking his mouth from hers, came down on top of her, his knee nudging her legs apart, his body sliding between them. Her blood beat in her ears, deafening her, silencing all her uncertainties and doubts. She had to have him, however much it cost; her body was aching and hot, needing him in it, hungering to take him inside herself. She had never in her life felt such intense need. It terrified her, but it was so strong that it drowned out everything but that sensual clamour. He pulled her belt free and her robe fell open; his hands slid inside it a second later, and she gave a moan of pleasure as she felt him touch her naked breast. Her skin was on fire instantly, her body arching in response.

He lifted his head to look down at her, his grey eyes half hooded by their drooping lids. He was darkly flushed, breathing rapidly as his stare explored her body: her pale throat and shoulders; the small, bud-like breasts, their skin so soft, except where the dark pink nipple rose out of a shadowed circle; the smooth creamy curve of her hips; her slim thighs and what lay between.

She couldn't bear to have him look at her; how could he miss the flaws she knew so well from her frenzied examinations of herself in mirrors? She winced as she thought of all the things that were wrong with her body.

'Don't look at me!' she cried out, putting her arms round his neck to pull him down towards her again, to stop him seeing her.

He buried his mouth between her breasts, whispering between kisses, 'I love to look at you—you're beautiful. I dream about your body.' He turned his head and took one of the hard pink aroused nipples into his mouth, sucked softly at it, and she closed her eyes, groaning.

The pleasure was so intense it was like dying, a crescendo of desire rising through her.

Gerard whispered, 'Do you dream about me, Keira?'

Why go on pretending? Her responses were betraying the truth anyway. 'Yes—oh, God, yes,' she moaned and feverishly began undoing his shirt, almost ripping the silky material because her hands were shaking so much.

Gerard kicked off the rest of his clothes, kissing her fiercely, his mouth hot but his body cool and smooth against hers once he was naked, their legs tangling, skin on skin; she felt the rough caress of body hair, the heat and moisture between her thighs as she ached for him to fill her.

'Are you on the Pill?' he asked hoarsely, kissing her navel, his tongue inserted into it, softly licking the concentric rings above the centre, following them round and round.

'Not at the moment. I haven't bothered for ages; I haven't been sleeping with anyone.' She was softly biting his shoulder, inhaling the scent of his body. His skin tasted and smelt faintly musky, very male, with overtones of pine-fragranced soap.

Suddenly it dawned on her why he had asked that question and she whispered, 'It doesn't matter!' Nothing mattered but finally satisfying her craving for him. She was going crazy; she needed him; she couldn't bear to let anything stop them making love tonight.

'Of course it matters!' he said impatiently. He shifted away to lean down towards the floor, where he had flung his clothes.

'What are you doing?' Frustration ate at her; was he going to get dressed again?

He was fumbling in his jacket; he swung his body up on to the bed again, and she saw what he held in his hand. A little jab of rage hit her. 'You planned this! You came prepared!'

He looked into her angry green eyes. 'I've had this in my pocket for a couple of days—I hoped we'd sleep together at my Tangier hotel after lunch yesterday.' His smile mocked her. 'We almost did, too.'

Her skin burnt with shame. 'You...you...' she stammered.

His eyes glittered with aroused excitement. 'Oh, come on, Keira! You knew I was dying to get to bed with you, and you were dying for it too—so can we stop pretending? We're both adults; we don't need anyone's permission to do what we badly want to do. Where's the problem?'

She closed her eyes. 'I'm scared,' she whispered, and felt his body tense.

'Why?'

'I don't know...'

His fingers smoothed along her mouth, parted her lips. 'You must know—talk to me, Keira, tell me what's on your mind. Do you think I don't realise you have real problems with relationships? It helps to talk about it. I'm not your analyst, but I want to know all about you.'

She took a deep breath, started, 'I want...' But she couldn't say it and fell silent again.

'Me,' he said softly. 'Me, Keira?'

She nodded, her eyes still tight shut.

'So what's stopping you? What are you afraid of?'

With a gasp she got it out. 'Loving...'

'Loving?' His voice was thoughtful.

'Loving too much.' It hurt to say it; she felt ill afterwards. She had given herself away, let him see inside her head; the intimacy of that was terrifying.

'Can you love too much?' he said quietly. 'Who says how much is too much? I love you like hell already and I seem to love you more every day. When do I start to call a halt? When do I say to myself, That's enough; don't love her any more?'

She had stopped listening; she was trembling violently. 'You...you said...you love...'

'You, Keira; I love you.' His voice was deep, charged. 'I knew it would happen, that day I broke in here and found you looking like a broken doll on the floor. I hardly knew you then; I'd been looking at you for months, staring because you were so lovely, but determined not to let myself get into another painful relationship. I always sensed I would fall for you if I ever got to know you. And I did. At once. It was like falling down a big black hole. You were so fragile, as light as a child when I carried you in here that day; I almost felt that if I let go of you you'd float, not fall down. You moved me. Scared me. Fascinated me. And every day the feeling gets stronger. I already love you more than I did yesterday, twice as much as I did last week...'

Tears were creeping out under her lids. He stroked her cheek, ran a finger over her closed eyes, gently wiping away the tears from her lashes, and she opened them to look at him, drowning in passion.

'I was in love with you before we met,' she whispered huskily. 'I fell in love with you on TV, before you came to live next door. When Sara insisted on inviting you to our party, that first time, and you didn't turn up, I wanted to kill you because I'd been so excited about meeting you at last. But...' She stopped, biting her lip, and he watched her, frowning.

'For God's sake, what is it, Keira? Is it so hard to tell me?'

'I don't want to scare you off!'

'You aren't an axe murderer, are you?' He was trying to lighten the atmosphere and she tried to laugh back at him.

'Worse,' she said. 'I ... I get too serious; I fall in love too hard ... I scared my last boyfriend off.'

He frowned again, his eyes intent on her face. 'He told you so? What a fool. But can't you see that it was just as well? He was obviously the wrong man for you. You made a mistake, Keira; you fell for someone who couldn't give you what you need, didn't want what you could give him.'

'I worked that out, eventually, but it didn't make it any easier. I still react in the same way to any sort of rejection.'

'The way you did when you lost that modelling contract?'

She nodded. 'The feelings well up ... I can't stop them.'

'So you eat? I've worked that out, Keira; why do you think I came straight here from the airport? I guessed how you'd react to your stepfather getting nasty with you. I'm beginning to know you very well. You need me, darling. I'm the right man for you—you should be grateful to that other guy. Because he was wise enough to walk away from you, you waited for me.' He pushed the tangle of red hair back from her face, looking passionately into her eyes. 'And I need all the love you've got; you couldn't give me too much—I need it all.'

She groaned, her arms going round his neck. 'Oh, darling ... even if you don't really mean it, that's a lovely thing to say.' Love had been a mirage in the desert of her life since she was a small child. She was afraid to believe that this time it was real.

He framed her flushed face between his hands and looked deep into her green eyes, his face intent and serious.

'I can see I'm going to be spending a lot of time in bed convincing you I really love you.'

She laughed huskily, and then a shudder ran through her as his hands slid downwards, warm and compelling, in slow, sensuous exploration.

'Starting now,' Gerard whispered, and she closed her eyes and stopped thinking, stopped questioning, as her body surrendered to the wild hunger which had torn at her from the first minute she ever saw him.

If you are looking for more titles by

CHARLOTTE LAMB

Don't miss these fabulous stories by one of
Harlequin's great authors:

Harlequin Presents®

#11480	SHOTGUN WEDDING	$2.89	☐
#11560	SLEEPING PARTNERS	$2.99	☐
#11584	FORBIDDEN FRUIT	$2.99	☐
#11618	DREAMING	$2.99	☐
#11706	GUILTY LOVE	$2.99 U.S.	☐
		$3.50 CAN.	☐
#11733	BODY AND SOUL	$3.25 U.S.	☐
		$3.75 CAN.	☐
#11743	DYING FOR YOU	$3.25 U.S.	☐
		$3.75 CAN.	☐
#11763	DARK FATE	$3.25 U.S.	☐
		$3.75 CAN.	☐

(limited quantities available on certain titles)

TOTAL AMOUNT	$
POSTAGE & HANDLING	$
($1.00 for one book, 50¢ for each additional)	
APPLICABLE TAXES*	$_____
TOTAL PAYABLE	$_____

(check or money order—please do not send cash)

To order, complete this form and send it, along with a check or money order
for the total above, payable to Harlequin Books, to: **In the U.S.:** 3010 Walden
Avenue, P.O. Box 9047, Buffalo, NY 14269-9047; **In Canada:** P.O. Box 613,
Fort Erie, Ontario, L2A 5X3.

Name: _____

Address: _____ City: _____

State/Prov.: _____ Zip/Postal Code: _____

*New York residents remit applicable sales taxes.
 Canadian residents remit applicable GST and provincial taxes.   HCLBACK7

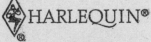

HARLEQUIN®

Look us up on-line at: http://www.romance.net

HARLEQUIN  PRESENTS®

PENNY JORDAN

"Penny Jordan pens a formidable read."
—*Romantic Times*

Harlequin brings you the best books by the best authors!

Watch for:
#1839 THE TRUSTING GAME

Christa had learned the hard way that men were not to be
trusted. So why should she believe Daniel when he said he
could teach her to trust?

Harlequin Presents—the best has just gotten better!
Available in October wherever
Harlequin books are sold.

Look us up on-line at: http://www.romance.net

HARLEQUIN PRESENTS®

For your eyes only!

Dear Reader,

re: SWEET SINNER by Diana Hamilton
   Harlequin Presents #1841

Zoe's boss, James, had formed the worst possible impression of Zoe and branded her a heartless tramp. Could she ever convince him that he was *so* wrong?

Yours sincerely,

The Editor at Harlequin Mills & Boon

P.S. Harlequin Presents—the best has just gotten better! Available in October wherever Harlequin books are sold.

P.P.S. Look us up on-line at: http://www.romance.net